Abigail's Arra

Book 5 in Clover Cre

Kirsten Osbourne

Forward:

I wrote this how it would be best for the story. The closest cattle market at the time this book is set (1853) to Clover Creek would have been Sacramento, California. The journey would have taken many months and have been extremely dangerous for our heroes.

Instead of keeping true to history, I have written this as a cattle drive to Idaho Falls, which wasn't really established until 1864. I felt like this information needed to be pointed out so people wouldn't look it up and tell me I was writing something that couldn't have happened.

This is fiction, and I'm making the place they travel to a real place that wasn't established yet. That's part of my fiction!

I hope you enjoy Bastian and Abby's story!

Dedication:

I want to dedicate this book to the real-life pioneers who built up this small area of what would be Idaho. The town I write about changed its name, and is now referred to as Montpelier, Idaho, which is the town I live in. The history here is apparent in every direction you look, and I am thankful that so many took the time to preserve the history.

Chapter One

Abigail Lund wanted to cry when she heard they were stopping for the evening. Most of the women on the trail were exhausted and ready to stop. And she was ready as well, but she knew her father would be in a horrible mood. He had been since her mother passed the month before. And one of their last four oxen had died earlier that day. Surely, he would find a way to blame it on Abby. He always did.

As the men parked the wagons for the night, Abby immediately went to start a fire. It had been a long hard day that had begun with the frightening descent of Big Hill.

Fortunately, no one had been killed in the descent and only one person had been injured, so they were all counting that as a win. She wished they'd been lucky enough to have a doctor along with them, but that hadn't happened. When she'd broken her arm early in the journey, it hadn't been set quite right, and it still pained her. She was just thankful it was an arm and not a leg.

She began cooking their meal, having gotten a roast from her friend Anna, whose husband had shot a buffalo the day before. Oh, they typically always shared meat with everyone, but sometimes when it was scarce, only close friends got some of the bounty.

She chopped the meat into tiny pieces and put it into the pot, covering it with water, while she peeled carrots and potatoes, and then dropped them in as well. Hopefully, the meal would please her father and put him in a better mood for a change.

He joined her just as she was sitting back after putting everything on to cook. "When do we eat?" he asked, his voice gruff.

"It should take an hour or so," Abby said, not meeting his gaze. He always seemed angrier when she looked at him.

"We lost another ox today," he said. "That leaves us with just two, and there will be no one to give the oxen a break. It's too much for them to walk every day."

"Is there no one who has extra we could buy?" she asked softly, praying he wouldn't be angered that she'd asked a question.

"Where are we going to get the money for oxen, girl? Use your head! God didn't put it on your shoulders to hold your hat!"

Abby nodded slightly. "Sorry, Pa."

"We're supposed to be near the town of Clover Creek the next couple of nights. I may see if we have anything someone needs in trade." He eyed her for a moment as if thinking about what he could see. "I could trade you for four oxen. I don't know that you're worth that much, but if you keep your mouth shut while we're there, I bet I could find someone to take you."

She didn't argue with him. It wouldn't be any use. Besides, she needed to be away from him. Perhaps being traded for oxen would be just what she needed to get away from his anger.

"All right, Pa."

He laughed, a good belly laugh. "I figured you'd agree. Your ma would never have agreed to it, but she was certain you were a good daughter who would do anything for her parents. I'm not so sure." He kicked her with the toe of his boot. "Just get supper done, and I'll see if anyone in the company will trade some oxen for you. If not, we'll find someone at the next settlement."

She rubbed her bottom where he'd kicked her as he walked away. They were parked beside Anna and her husband, and Anna hurried over. "Are you all right? I saw him kick you!"

Abigail shrugged. "It's not the hardest he's kicked me, nor the first time. Hopefully, it will be the last."

"What do you mean?" Anna asked. She and Abigail had been friends before Anna married, and they set out on the trail.

"Just that he's trying to find someone to trade four oxen for me. He said if no one in the company will do it, he'll sell me to someone in the next settlement we reach, Clover Creek. We'll be there tomorrow." Abigail kept her voice light as if being sold to a stranger for cows was something that happened every day.

"Oh, Abby...I wish I knew what to say. I don't want to see you sold to a stranger, and there aren't many young unmarried men looking for wives in our company."

"There's old Mr. Schuster," Abby said, but she knew she would never be able to marry the old man. His wife had died at the beginning of their journey, and she'd been forty years younger than him. She was raising her children and his previous wife's children. Now he had to deal with the children on his own. Several times he'd tried to approach her and ask her to "step out" with him, but she'd always said no. Thankfully, she didn't think he had enough oxen to spare.

"You are not marrying him!" Anna hissed at her. "You're not marrying anyone like him either. I refuse to lose my best friend to marriage to an old man."

"I don't know that I have a lot of choice in the matter," Abby said. Her mother had always let her make her own decisions, but her father had never done so. He'd been mean to her mother, but she'd never seen him raise his hand to her. He had always looked at Abby as a wasted piece of human flesh to pound on and kick.

"Oh, Abby. I can't lose you!"

Abby nodded, a tear slowly descending her face. "If I marry someone in the town we're about to reach, then I'll just have to write to you."

Anna nodded, tears filling her eyes. "And I'll write you back!"

"I know you will. If I stay, we'll talk Steven into coming back here to live. I'm sure there's still land around. Look at that vast prairie!"

"And if we're only a day's walk from Clover Creek now, we'll be close enough to take a horse even if we live here. And your father won't be able to stop us."

Abby smiled. "Has he ever?"

Anna giggled, thinking of some of the mischief she and Abby had gotten up to over the years of their friendship. They'd only fought once, and that was because Abby had a crush on Steven, but he'd only ever had eyes for Anna.

Abby had forgotten her crush on her friend's husband a few years before, and now they were as thick as thieves. At nineteen, they were old enough to go to Oregon and claim their own territory, but it didn't seem as if Abby would make it all the way to Oregon.

Supper was ready when her father returned. "Only man who'll have you is old man Schuster, but he only has one spare ox, and he needs that one to make it to Oregon. Hopefully, we'll be able to trade you in Clover Creek." He took the bowl Abby handed him and said a long prayer over the meal. He was proud of what a good Christian he was and took every opportunity to show it.

After the meal, he wandered off again. He only spent time with her if he needed something from her, so Abby mostly felt she was on the Trail by herself. Well, with Anna and Steven really. When her mother had been alive it was different, but now, without her mother, she was really and truly alone.

Abby scrubbed the dishes clean and put all of their cooking utensils into the wagon. Her father hadn't said a single thing about the stew. At least with her mother, he'd always grunted that the food was good. With her, it was as if he was afraid if he complimented her, she'd want to stay with him.

They only had half a day's walk to Clover Creek the following day, and they camped in a large area at the base of a huge hill. Many of the women had gone to the store in the small town to shop, but Abby knew they didn't have the money to waste on frivolities like fresh bacon when there were plenty of beans left for them to eat.

She was in the process of starting her cookfire for the night when her pa walked up behind her with a young man beside him. "Abby, this is Bastian."

"What an odd name!" she said, nervous because she was sure this man was trading four oxen for her.

He nodded. "It's Sebastian, but my younger sister started calling me Bastian as soon as she could talk, so now I'm Bastian."

"I like that. Are you close to your sister?" she asked.

Her pa drew his foot back, but then seemed to think better of it. "You need to hush while we men work some details out."

Abby nodded, not much caring what was said at that moment. She was just happy she'd not been kicked.

The men walked away and talked for a few minutes, but when Pa came back, he looked positively gleeful. "He's trading six oxen for you. I told him that he was overvaluing you, but he insisted."

"I see." Not that she was at all surprised. She'd expected it. "Should I stay here and fix supper for you, or do you want me to leave now?"

Pa seemed to think about it for a minute, but he finally said, "I'll walk with the two of you to the church. I'm not going to trade you to be a whore. He said he'd marry you."

Abby wasn't surprised by his words, but Bastian gasped. "You can't call her a whore!"

Pa looked confused about why the other man was upset. "Oh, I didn't. I said she'd be a wife, not a whore."

Abby didn't say anything, but she stood and gathered the belongings that were hers and not the family's. She had two dresses, a journal her ma had given her, and her mother's necklace. Nothing else. She refused to feel ashamed about how little she had. "I have to tell my friend Anna."

Bastian nodded, understanding women's friendships were different than men's. "Go."

Abby ran to Anna's wagon and quickly explained she was marrying a man named Bastian.

"I'll miss you! And I'll nag Steven every day until he agrees for us to settle here."

Abby laughed softly as she hugged her friend goodbye. "I sure do hope we'll see you soon." And with those words, she ran back to walk a few steps behind her father and Bastian to the church.

Bastian kept looking over his shoulder at her, as if he thought she should walk with him, but she seemed to prefer her spot behind them. It was odd to him, but he also thought it was odd that he'd been able to buy her for six oxen.

Thankfully Pa had married a year before, and he had a cabin of his own. It wasn't large, but it was big enough for two. Eventually, they'd build him a house, but his married siblings came first. One of his brothers had just moved into a house of his own earlier that summer.

Bastian called out when they arrived at the church, which was also the parsonage. "Pastor Scott! Mrs. Scott!"

A young woman who couldn't have been more than a year or two older than Abby walked into the sanctuary. When she saw who was yelling, she smiled. "How can I help you, Bastian?"

"I'm here to get married. Is the pastor around anywhere?"

"Yes, I'll go get him. He's just outside." Mrs. Scott hurried away, and came back with a man who was wearing work clothes, and had sweat streaming down his face.

"Sorry, I was out chopping up some wood for winter."

Bastian nodded. "It's not much fun, but it needs to happen. I'm here to marry Abigail."

The pastor turned his gaze to Abby. "You must be from the wagon train that just set up camp."

Abby nodded, knowing better than to say much with her father there. He'd kick her if he felt she was speaking out of turn.

"If you don't mind my appearance and smell, we can do it right now."

"We don't mind," Bastian answered, talking for both of them.

Pastor Scott looked at her father. "You must be Abigail's father."

"Unfortunately," the man said, surprising both the pastor and Abby's future husband.

"I think we're ready," Abby said, smiling as brightly as she could.

The pastor nodded, turning all his attention to the couple before him. He led them through simple vows, and invited Bastian to kiss his bride at the end.

Bastian looked at her as if she had just crawled out from under a rock, but finally, he leaned down and kissed her. It was just a peck on her lips, but it was good enough. She was married.

Pa stood and shook the pastor's hand. "Goodbye, girl. Be obedient to your husband." He said nothing else as he left the church and headed back to camp.

Bastian looked at Abby. "My wagon is over by the general store, but it's not a long walk. We'll go get it and drive to my house at the top of the hill."

Abby nodded. "Yes, sir."

"I'm not a sir. Just a Bastian," he said, holding the door for her.

"People call me Abby," she said softly. She wished she understood why he'd given her such an odd look when he was told to kiss her, but she thrust the thought from her mind. She would be the best wife he could ask for. He'd traded six oxen for her after all.

As they walked toward the store, she asked, "Do you have family nearby?"

He nodded. "Yup."

When he didn't elaborate, she smiled. He seemed a bit awkward to her, but she liked him. "Who is close?"

"My pa, my two brothers and their wives, and my sister and her husband. Kids."

"I see. Did you lose your mother?"

He shook his head. "Nope, we know just where she's buried on the trail."

Abby blinked a few times. He wasn't joking about the death of his mother, was he? Surely not. "I know where mine is buried as well," she finally said, unsure what else to say.

"I don't like your pa," Bastian said after a moment of silence.

She smiled. It was nice to know her husband was good at reading people. "He's a good man but never much cared for me."

"I could tell. He told me you were only worth four oxen, but I said I wouldn't give less than six. He needed the oxen, and I needed a wife. My sister and sisters-in-law have been cooking for me for far too long."

"There aren't any young ladies in town?" she asked.

"Not that don't know me."

She wasn't sure if she'd misheard him, but she let it go. Life with Bastian was going to be interesting, to say the least.

Chapter Two

When they'd reached the general store, Bastian asked Abby, "Is there anything you need to get? I don't keep anything for food preparation in my cabin. My sister, stepmom, and sisters-in-law take turns having me over for meals, so I don't have to worry about that at all."

"That's nice! Am I right to think you can't cook?"

Bastian shrugged. "I can do a couple of meals, but I don't like it. I figure a six-oxen wife can do the cooking."

Abby smiled. "I'm happy to cook. But I'm surprised you insisted on paying two extra oxen for me. Pa would have taken two oxen if you'd tried to barter with him."

Bastian shook his head. "You're worth a lot more than two oxen or even six oxen. I think your father is being very short-sighted to get rid of you, unless he already has his eyes on a widow."

"Pa doesn't like people enough to even court a woman, let alone marry another. I don't know why he and Ma married, but whatever it was, everything was over as soon as she died." Abby took a deep breath. "I wasn't allowed to mourn her. If he saw me crying, he kicked me."

"Well, I won't be treating you that way. We'll talk about all that after we shop. Don't worry about vegetables or meats. We're covered there. But we'll need things like flour and sugar, and all the other things a kitchen needs."

"All right," she said. She followed him into the store, and he walked straight to the counter. Instead of following Bastian, Abby made a mental list of what she'd need as a wife. When she spotted some pretty red and white gingham, she decided to ask Bastian if he had curtains and a tablecloth. She could make something perfect with just a few yards of fabric.

Bastian walked back to Abby. "You're thinking about something."

Abby smiled. "I am. I was wondering if you had curtains and a tablecloth. I could make something nice out of this red gingham."

"I don't. Never felt the need."

"What is my budget?" she asked. Her pa had never let her step foot into a store without telling her how much she could spend. Surely, Bastian would feel the same.

Bastian looked at her for a moment. "I just set it up with the owner for you to have credit here. You tell him what we need, and it'll be taken care of."

She eyed him skeptically. "I'm sure you don't want me to buy too much though. A budget would really help me."

He thought about it for a moment. "Keep it under five hundred dollars. That's the amount the Jensens' owe us for providing and delivering meat to them and some of their customers. We never use all the credit we have here."

Abby's jaw dropped at the amount of money. "I don't think I could spend that much if I tried!"

He shrugged. "Spend it or someone else in the family will. But we're always doing business with Jensen, and he won't mind if we owe him a little, because he'll end up using the credit up for more beef. And chickens. And goat cheese."

"Oh my!" She'd had no idea what Bastian did, but it sounded like he raised a lot of different animals. Since she didn't know how often he'd bring her into town, she ordered all she needed.

Walking to the man behind the counter, she said, "I need fifty pounds of flour, twenty-five pounds of sugar, ten pounds of brown sugar, six yards of the red gingham..." Her list went on from there. The man just nodded and got what she'd asked for.

When it was time to cut the fabric, he frowned. "My wife, Penelope, usually cuts the yard goods for me, but she's home with a sick baby. I have no idea how to do it."

Abby smiled. "You measure it out, and I'll cut it."

"Thank you. I'll give you a penny off per yard for doing the work for me."

She was happy to be able to save some of the money she was spending on her order. It made her feel that she would be less of a burden to Bastian and his family. She hoped his sister and sisters-in-law were kind people. It was definitely what she needed after saying goodbye to her best friend since childhood.

After the wagon had been loaded by Mr. Jensen, Bastian helped her up, and climbed into the wagon himself. "We're not far from here, but the hill is steep, so we typically bring the wagon down when we need to buy anything. Just makes things easier all around."

"Sounds good," Abby said, thankful that he wasn't demanding anything from her or berating her in any way. She'd almost forgotten what it was like to be treated like she was valued. Her mother had only been gone for one month, but it had been a long, hard month.

He drove up a hill on a road that had been forged by wagons over the years the settlement had been there, stopping near the top. He hurried around the wagon and helped her down. "I'll show you around, but I have to be quick about it. My father and brothers expected me back a long time ago. They hate it when I get distracted and don't do everything I'm supposed to do."

He carried in the flour and sugar for her. "You'll have to unload the rest. No time."

She nodded. There wasn't much to the cabin, and she didn't need him to show her around. There was a kitchen and dining area, a bedroom, and a loft. What was there to see? She was grateful for every square inch of space after so long on the trail though. They'd left April fifteenth, and it was already September fifteenth. She couldn't wait for him to leave so she could sit on a bed and remember what mattresses felt like.

"You can go," she said softly. "I'll show myself around."

Bastian nodded. "Supper at five," he said as he headed for the door. She was surprised he'd left so abruptly, but Bastian didn't seem like other men.

As soon as he was gone, she explored the small house, wondering if she was supposed to sleep upstairs or in the bedroom with him. Either way, she needed to get the wagon unloaded and start supper.

So, she carried in each of her purchases, setting the food in the kitchen area. There was a handle on the floor that she was certain led down to the cellar. Hopefully, there would be some food down there, but if not, she'd wander until she found someone who could help her. Bastian had said the whole family lived close. What were the chances she could knock on all the doors and not find either a member of his family, or someone who could point her to a relative of his?

As soon as she had stored everything where she wanted it, and laid on the bed for just a moment, wondering if she was going to be spoiled by the sheer comfort of it, she wandered outside. Around two hundred yards away was another cabin much like the one she was in. She decided to try it first.

She walked to the cabin and knocked, waiting patiently for someone to hear her. She could hear laughter from inside the house, and she certainly hoped she was in the right place. Laughter was exactly what she needed in life.

A pretty brunette with a well-rounded belly came to the door, her face lit up by the smile that reached her eyes. "Hello."

Abby couldn't help but smile back. "Hello. I married Bastian a couple of hours ago, and he said his sisters-in-law and his sister would have food for me to fix for supper."

"That's wonderful! I'm Fiona."

"I'm Abigail, but my friends call me Abby."

"Abby it is." Fiona looked over her shoulder. "Bastian's wife is here!" There were suddenly three other women peeking at her. "I'm Henri, Bastian's sister."

"I'm Emma, Bastian's brother Jared's wife," said another woman with beautiful dark hair.

"I'm Melody, Bastian's stepmother. I married into the family just a bit over a year ago."

"I hope there won't be a quiz!" Abby said, glad to see that the women were used to working together. She didn't know what they'd been doing, but there had been laughter involved, and she had a sudden longing to be accepted into the lives these women shared.

"Where are my manners?" Fiona asked. "Come in! Come in! Did you arrive with the other emigrants who are camping here tonight?"

Fiona nodded. "I did." For a moment, she struggled for an explanation, but she decided the truth was the simplest thing. "My father traded me to Bastian for six oxen."

Henri looked enraged. "Your father sold you? And Bastian bought you? How could anyone think that was all right?"

"Truthfully, I was happy Bastian was willing to be the one to trade for me. My father hasn't been himself since my mother died a month ago."

Fiona shook her head. "No one is happy when their spouse dies, but as far as I know, you're the only one to be traded for oxen." She waved her hand toward the table. "Take a seat. We're just putting up some green beans. Don't worry, you'll get your share."

"I didn't help grow them!" Abby protested.

Henri smiled. "I didn't help at all with the growing last summer, and I still got all my family needed. I was expecting, and it was too much for me."

Fiona nodded. "And I was expecting all winter, and the girls helped me out a great deal. We're family now, and we're helping each other."

After a moment of consideration, Abby nodded. "Thank you."

"You're so welcome!" Emma said, scooping some of the beans into a jar.

The women obviously had a system because they worked together very efficiently. When a baby cried from the other room, Melody said, "That would be my baby." She handed Abby the rag she'd been holding. "Your turn."

Abby quickly took her new mother-in-law's spot in the assembly line. It was amazing to her that they already trusted her to help, but then again, there were four of them and one of her. What could she possibly do to derail the process?

While they worked, the women laughed and joked. They had so much to say, it was as if they'd been apart for months. "Do you work together often?" Abby asked when there was a lull in the conversation.

Henri laughed. "Every day, usually. It's just so much nicer to have friends around. Emma and Fiona have the biggest homes, but we travel to them all at one time or another."

"Why do you move from home to home?" Abby asked.

"More fun that way," Emma said with a grin. "When we're not gardening, we're cleaning and cooking, so we just do it all together. I don't think any of us planned this when we started out, but it works beautifully. We scrubbed every inch of Fiona's home this morning before we started canning. Tomorrow, we're all going to Melody's, and that's really where we should do all the canning. She has a nice big kitchen with a real cookstove."

"Which house is Melody's?" Abby asked. "And may I come along?"

"Of course!" Emma said. "You're family, and even if we're just sewing, we can talk as we go along, and it keeps the loneliness at bay."

"I think marrying Bastian may have been the best thing I could have done."

Melody walked in then. "It has to be," she said with a smile. "It was the best thing for me as well." She snuggled her baby close, sitting in a chair so she could easily nurse.

"Where are you from?" Fiona asked Abby. "We all know each other. Tell us why you were on the Trail!"

"I just turned eighteen and was still living with my parents when my pa decided we were going west. The doctor warned Pa that Ma was too sick to make the trip, but he wouldn't listen, so I agreed to take care of Ma and do as much of her work as possible. She died last month, and I've been taking care of my pa since, but he never much cared for me. I'd rather the whole town didn't know I was sold for six oxen, but at least Bastian talked him up from four to six."

Henri laughed. "Only Bastian would negotiate in the other direction, but I think he's right. You're more of a six oxen wife than a four."

Even Abby had to laugh at that. "Oh, and I'm from Pennsylvania."

Emma smiled. "The men are ranching here, but we've made them add more and more animals for us to take care of as we've gone along. We have chickens, goats, horses, cattle, hogs, and even a kitten or two."

"Oh, do you think I could pick an animal?"

Henri laughed. "I don't know how many animals are left with all we have. And the men do serious hunting in the fall, so we also have a lot of game."

Emma nodded. "Mainly my brother Roy. He's an amazing hunter. Seriously, he can hunt anything."

"Turkeys?" Abby suggested. "I know nothing about them, but I could raise turkeys!"

The other women all exchanged a look and laughed. "Turkeys sound great," Emma said. "I don't believe anyone in town raises them, but wild turkeys are always running around. We'll see if Roy can set up a trap that will catch a couple but not kill them."

Abby smiled. If she had some way to contribute to this family, she would feel much better about herself. "I love a good turkey dinner!"

Henri nodded. "I do as well, and it gets tiring to ask Roy to go shoot another all the time. Better to raise them."

"I have a question..."

They all turned their attention to Abby the assembly line stopping completely. "When I asked Bastian if there weren't girls around who he could marry, he said, 'Not ones who don't know me.' Which made me wonder why he'd say such a thing!"

Henri looked at her. "I'm probably the best one to answer that. Bastian is a bit odd. He's funny and fun to be around but seems a little slow in some ways. He doesn't really know how to talk to women or be charming, for example."

Abby nodded. If that's all it was, she could certainly work with that. It was good to know he didn't have a checkered past.

Chapter Three

When it was time to head home for supper, Abby was given chicken, carrots, and potatoes, two of the few vegetables Bastian would eat. At least they were according to Henri who seemed to know everything about her brothers.

She hurried home and fried up the chicken and put the potatoes on to boil. The carrots cooked in a small pot as well. She was surprised at how well-equipped Bastian's bachelor kitchen was, but she was definitely pleased by it. It was so easy to make a meal. If only she had a stove like Fiona's, she would be in heaven.

While she cooked, she took stock of the cabin, and found that she'd landed in much better circumstances than she would have if she'd completed her journey to Oregon City. Here, she was the mistress of her own home, and she didn't have to deal with her father's moods. No, this was right where she wanted to be.

Once the potatoes had been boiled and the chicken was fried, she made some gravy from the drippings. She'd seen a big, beautiful stove at the store that day, and it was less than one hundred dollars. Surely, he wouldn't mind buying that for her with all he'd offered.

When Bastian came in at the end of his day, he sniffed deeply. "Something smells good!"

Abby smiled. "I made fried chicken and mashed potatoes. I hope you'll like it."

"Anything is better than cooking for myself." He washed his hands from the pitcher on the counter and sat down at the table. "How much longer?"

She pulled the gravy off the stove. "This is the last thing. I didn't get around to baking bread, but I did help put up some green beans for winter."

He nodded. "I knew you were worth six oxen."

Abby wasn't certain if she should be flattered or offended, so she let the comment go. "I didn't know if I should put my things in the loft or in the bedroom, so I put them in the bedroom, and I'll put them up in the loft if you'd prefer."

Bastian nodded, bowing his head to pray. He'd barely finished when there was a loud knock on the door.

He wiped his mouth on his napkin, walking to the door. He opened it wide to find his father and two brothers looking at him. "What's wrong?" he asked.

They all came into the house, and Pa was shaking his head. "You didn't think to tell us that you were late because you got married this afternoon?"

Bastian shrugged. "I was late. That's that."

There was a moment of silence as Abby wondered if Bastian would introduce them. When he didn't, she stood. "I'm Abby."

"Nice to meet you," the oldest of the three men said.

"Abby Appleby," another of them mused. "I'm Jared the oldest brother."

"I'm Sam, and I'm the middle brother," the third man said.

"Melody is whipping up a cake so we can at least have wedding cake to celebrate your wedding," Pa said. "Come up to the house after supper."

Bastian shrugged. "I think Abby needs to do dishes after supper."

"After the dishes are done then," Pa said, shaking his head. "You need to stop being so literal, boy."

"I just like things to make sense," Bastian replied.

"I want to raise turkeys," Abby said. "Everyone seems to have their own animal, and that's what I want to raise."

Pa shrugged. "Guess we're building another enclosure tomorrow, boys."

No one seemed to think much of her desire to raise turkeys. They just saw it as work to be done, which is how Abby thought it should be. Everyone should take the work they had and tackle it head on.

The men filed out of the house and Bastian and Abby returned to the table. "I wish you'd told your family we were married."

"Why?" he asked. "They know now."

She decided to leave that as it was. He certainly was different than most of the men she knew. "Do you want me to leave my clothes in your room?"

"Sure," he said. "Married people sleep together."

"Yes, they do," she said. She hadn't considered the idea of their wedding night, but he was a handsome man. She was certain they could muddle through it.

After she'd finished the dishes, they walked over to the big house, and had cake with the entire family. Even Henri's husband Roy was there to be a part of it. "This cake is delicious," Abby said after her first bite.

Roy sat on one side of Abby and Jared on the other. Abby had learned through conversations that day that Henri and Jared had married Roy and Emma, who were also brother and sister. She looked back and forth between them.

Roy took a bite of his cake. "I'm not sure Bastian knows what a wedding night is about," he said.

Jared nodded emphatically. "Don't be surprised if he runs screaming into the night. He does that sometimes."

The two men continued to tease her about Bastian, and as she finished her cake, she pushed it away. "Maybe you two should go bother someone else." She was getting annoyed with their behavior.

Henri noticed what was happening then. She grabbed Roy's arm and nodded to Emma to get Jared. "If he doesn't get a wedding night because of you, I'm going to smack you!" Emma said to Jared.

"I was just teasing," Jared said, looking down.

"Me too," Roy said, not sure if he should be apologizing or running from his wife. She was kind and sweet but had a temper, and he didn't want it directed at him.

"You both should be apologizing to Bastian!" Abby said, glaring at the two men.

The other women reminded Abby that she was to meet them at Melody's house the following morning, and she agreed. As they left the house, Abby was quiet, wondering what exactly Bastian was thinking. He was a man who liked to tease from what she'd been told, but he hadn't teased her at all.

They walked to the cabin, and he held the door for her. When they got inside, he looked at her for a moment. "So did the guys make you not want to have our wedding night?" he asked.

Abby smiled, walking to her new husband, prepared to let him do whatever he wanted. He'd traded six oxen for her after all. "It's our wedding night. We can't have it next month," she said.

He chuckled. "I'm glad the guys didn't bug you then. They don't mean to be idiots. It's just part of who they are."

She put her arms around his neck. "It's fine. Some men are just silly, that's all."

Bastian laughed, leaning down to kiss her. She'd never been kissed except the peck at her wedding, though she'd thought about it a lot especially when she'd talked with Anna. Anna had given her more information about what was supposed to happen on a wedding night than her mother ever had.

The kiss surprised her in its intensity. At the church, he'd seemed so shy when he'd kissed her, but now, he seemed to want to hurry things along. She couldn't blame him though. It was their wedding night after all.

She took his hand and led him into the bedroom, shutting the door behind her. "I'm glad you were the one to trade for me," she said softly.

"Me too. I thought you'd cook and clean, but here we are, about to consummate our marriage. I'm glad because I've wanted to do it for a long time."

She bit her lip to keep from laughing at the casual way he'd announced he'd wanted marital relations. She did find the way he was so forthright about everything very refreshing.

She reached out to unbutton his shirt, noting the surprise on his face. "Is it all right that I'm doing this?" she asked.

He nodded. "But I thought I was supposed to undress both of us."

"My married friend said she undresses her husband pretty often."

"Then I guess it's all right for you to undress me." He waited as she finished unbuttoning his shirt and it fell to the floor.

She stared at the vast expanse of his chest for a moment, surprised at the muscles she found but not entirely sure why. He was obviously a hard worker and ran a ranch with his father and brothers. Of course, he was strong.

He turned her around and unbuttoned the back of her dress, and she stepped out of it. She hadn't worn her corset since they had started out from Independence, Missouri, so she was a bit worried he wouldn't like how her waist had thickened during the long trek, but he made no complaints.

When she turned around to face him again in just her petticoat and drawers, it was strange, knowing he was looking at her as no man ever had before. She stood still and proud as he looked at her body, trailing one finger from her breast down to her waist.

"Cows only get big in their udders when they are milking. Why are women big there when they're not nursing a baby?"

Abby couldn't help but smile. "I'm not really sure why," she said.

"I like it," he said.

"I'm glad!" She moved closer to him, so she was pressed right up against him. "That feels nice."

"I think it would feel nicer if you weren't wearing any clothes," he said. With his words, he pushed the petticoat off her shoulders and then her knickers down to her feet. "There. Now I like you even better."

He pulled her to him so she was pressed right up against him, before lowering his head to kiss her. She put her arms around him, her hands exploring his back while they kissed.

"I think you should lie down now," he said. "I'll get my britches off for myself."

She couldn't stop the smile that transformed her face. He was a good man. She could feel it.

And then she could feel him. He spent a moment toying with her breast, and then he was atop her and inside her. She wasn't certain it was supposed to happen so quickly, but he seemed content and for that moment, that was enough for her. She wanted to please him, and when she heard his shout just before he rolled off her, she could only assume she had.

He kept one arm around her for a while, and then rolled with his back to her. "I don't like to be touching anyone while I sleep."

"That's all right," Abby said. She didn't care if she touched someone while she slept, but she was used to sleeping alone, so it didn't matter that he didn't like it.

She laid awake for a while, wishing she'd found the bliss that Anna had told her was part of the marriage act, but she was sure it would happen. Maybe the next time.

She woke before dawn as was her habit, and she went into the kitchen to fix breakfast. She'd forgotten that she had no eggs, so she hurried out to where she'd been told the chickens had their own area in the barn. There she found six eggs and carried them home.

She'd been fascinated by johnny cakes on the Trail, but she was sick of them now. She'd make some pancakes for breakfast. Everyone loved pancakes. As she was squatted in front of the fireplace cooking, she thought about the stove she wanted. She'd have to ask Bastian if she could have one after he woke.

When Bastian got up, he immediately went out to the barn. "I need to milk the cows," he said on his way out the door.

She had no time to respond or talk to him about anything. There was plenty of time, though. After watching him eat the night before, she had a feeling that Bastian never turned down a meal.

When he returned inside, the food was ready, and they sat and said a quick prayer. "I was wondering something," she said after she'd taken her first bite of pancakes. She couldn't believe how much she'd missed them.

"What's that?" he asked.

"I saw a cookstove in the store yesterday. Could I get one?"

He shrugged. "I don't see why not. I think all of the girls have one now."

"When?" she asked, hoping it would be soon. She could cook over an open fire easily, but she really missed the joy of cooking on a stove. It was so much easier.

"I'll get the men to go down with me today. We'll have it installed before supper."

"Thank you!" She was surprised he wasn't arguing with her, but she'd already determined that her new family was more affluent than her last had been.

"Sure. I don't mind at all. We do so much bartering in this valley that you always owe someone a favor, or they owe you one. With the store, they owe us."

"That's a good thing," she said.

He nodded. "It's best to use up the credit, or money will have to exchange hands at the end of the year. We have to pay taxes on money, but not when we barter."

"I never thought of that," she said.

"We're happy to pay taxes of course, but sometimes, it's nice not to have to." Bastian took another bite of pancakes. "This is delicious."

"I've missed pancakes. The corn flour lasted so much longer that we only had johnny cakes on the Trail."

"I got sick of johnny cakes, but I like them again now that we're not eating them most mornings. My sister is a fabulous cook, but you're good too. You were worth six oxen for sure, and maybe even eight."

"Thank you," Abby said, deciding to take any references to her worth oxen as compliments. What else could she do?

"What are your plans for the day?" he asked.

"We're all meeting at Melody's house," she said. "I don't remember what we're doing there, but I said I'd go. It seems the women work together most days."

He nodded. "Do you really want to raise turkeys?"

"I do. I love turkey and dressing."

"All right. I don't mind. But the children have to come first."

"The children?" she asked.

"The children we're going to have because we had a wedding night."

Abby smiled. "We will have children, I'm sure. I'm excited about it."

"Me too. But they have to be cared for properly. Do you know how to take care of a baby?" Bastian asked.

She nodded. "I do. I've never done it before, but I know how."

"You probably need to spend more time with the other women then. They'll show you."

"I'll do that."

Chapter Four

Emma stopped by while Abby was doing the breakfast dishes. She immediately took a towel to wipe them dry and helped out. "We're the only two without little ones who aren't expecting," Emma said. "How would you feel about going to the garden with me and picking peas before we head to Melody's this morning? I had planned to get the picking done after supper, but when Melody made the cake for your wedding, we had to go there instead."

"I'd be happy to help!" Abby said. "I want to contribute to the family. Especially since Bastian is getting me a cook stove today."

"Wonderful! It makes meals so much easier!" Emma said. "I have one too, but I live in a large house as well. Next summer, Fiona gets her house, and I guess you'll get yours the next summer."

Abby's eyes widened. "I'm happy with the cabin. I don't need something bigger!" The cabin was as big as the cabin she'd shared with her parents back East.

"Oh, you'll want a bigger house soon. Fiona told Sam she needed a cookstove when she agreed to marry him, so she's had one for over a year. It's your turn!"

"I was worried I was spending too much of the family's money."

Emma shook her head. "No, you're not. The Applebys were one of the wealthiest families to come West with us."

"Well, I'm happy to get that stove then. I'll try to be careful about what I spend."

Emma laughed. "I told Jared he needed to come home with ten dozen jars today. I'm not terribly worried about what I spend."

"Thank you for telling me that. It makes me feel a lot better about what I spend."

"Hey, we're sisters now. We have to share secrets, don't we?"

"I really like the way you think! Are we canning peas today?"

Emma nodded. "Hence the need to pick them." She wiped the last dish and put it away. "Are you ready?"

"Let me just grab my bonnet. Ma always warned me about how dark my face gets."

The two of them went to the garden together and picked the peas. It only took an hour and then they were at Melody's. Abby was given the job of shelling the peas while the others took care of other tasks. She didn't bother to pay attention to what the others did as she worked on the peas. She could follow orders and do her share without any problem.

Shortly after lunch that day, she realized she was laughing and joking along with the other women. If anyone were to come to the house as she had the day before, they would assume she'd known the other women for years. Oh, she was happy her father had traded her for six oxen. Maybe she hadn't enjoyed her marital relations yet, but she would. She was sure of it.

She was again given beef, potatoes, and carrots for their supper. Making a stew would be perfect, especially if she had her new stove. She couldn't wait to cook on it and not squat in front of the fire.

She even planned to make a loaf of bread for supper that night. Surely, Bastian would enjoy fresh bread.

When she got home, the cookstove was right where she'd told Bastian she wanted it. It was all ready for her to use, and she couldn't be happier with it.

She started a big pot of stew on the stove and then worked on mixing her bread dough. She wanted him to be happy with the meals she made.

As soon as he was home, she hurried to him and threw her arms around him, thanking him for the stove. "You have no idea how much this means to me!"

"It means your life is easier," Bastian said, looking at her as if she'd lost her mind.

"Yes, it does. So, thank you."

"You're welcome." He sat at the table. "What did you cook on your new stove?"

"Just stew and some bread." She hoped he wouldn't be disappointed.

"As long as it's not bear, I'll love it," he said.

"You don't like bear meat?" She'd eaten it often as a child but had never much cared for it. It would be nice if he didn't either; she wouldn't have to cook it.

"Not at all. Only Jared likes it, and I think that means he's insane."

She laughed. "I'm not fond of it either. Now I never have to put it on the table."

He smiled a little. "Thanks for that."

Once she had supper on the table and they were eating, he asked, "When are you making the curtains and the tablecloth?"

"It's harvest season. We're all working on harvesting the garden and putting up the foods for next year."

"So, when you're done with harvest?"

"Most likely. I didn't know I'd be so busy with the harvest when I bought the fabric."

He shrugged. "I don't care either way, I just thought you wanted to get it done soon."

"Not when I can be harvesting and contributing to our food for next year."

He nodded. "All right. Do you like pie?" he asked.

"Pie? I love pie. Emma said I could have some of the raspberry pie filling they put up last month if I wanted it."

"Yes, please," he said. "I live for pie. I love chicken pot pie, and turkey pie, and beef pie, and cherry pie, and apple pie...I love pie!"

"There are still blackberries to pick from the garden, and Fiona said some apple trees are near her father's house. I would happily go pick some."

He smiled. "Apple trees?"

"I'll make sure I get there this week. They should all be ripe!"

"Week is over," he said. "Tomorrow is Sunday. Your company is still camped here. I heard they plan to attend church in the morning."

"Oh, it'll be nice to have a chance to say goodbye then," Abby said. Saying goodbye to Anna would be hard, but they'd already done it once, so surely, they could do it again.

She wished she felt as if she could give her friend food to help her on their journey, but she couldn't take food from her new family to give away. It wouldn't be right.

Then she had a thought. "Could I invite my friend and her husband for Sunday dinner?" She knew she could get plenty of food from the other women.

He shrugged. "Sure. I wouldn't mind."

"Then I'll do that. I'm going to leave the dishes for a minute or two and run over to talk to Fiona about what I can make."

"All right. I'm going to keep eating." Bastian cut himself another slice of bread and applied butter to it.

Abby all but ran to Fiona's cabin and asked about food. "Oh, sure! I have some salt pork that would work well or if you want something a little fancier, I could spare a chicken or beef."

"Anything," Abby said. "I'm a beggar, and I'll be happy to take what you give me."

Fiona smiled. "Let me look then." Abby stepped inside and waited while Fiona found something. Sam was sitting at the table still eating.

"I'm sorry to disturb your supper!" Abby said.

"Don't worry about it," Sam said.

Fiona hurried back to her. "Two pieces of salt pork. It should be more than enough for four, and you can do what you want with it.

When we got off the trail, all my family cared about was not eating more beans!"

Abby laughed. "Just a few days ago I was telling my friend, Anna, that if I had to eat beans even one more time, I might have to hurt someone."

Fiona nodded emphatically. "I can eat them again, but they still don't make me happy. I used to love nights when we had beans."

As Abby walked back home, she thought about what she'd make with the salt pork. Of course, her friend wouldn't care one way or the other. She didn't have to cook and would have something other than beans. Anna wouldn't care about anything else.

Bastian had just finished eating when she got home, and she immediately started the dishes. To her surprise, Bastian found a book on horse training and sat at the table reading it while she worked. "Are you interested in horse training?" she asked.

He looked up from the book, his face lit up. "I am. I want to teach them how to behave themselves and start selling them. We have lots more horses than we need and a good stallion. Several good mares. We only use geldings to work on the ranch, so we do not need to keep them other than to breed. Thank goodness Doc doesn't mind working on animals. Some doctors think animal care is beneath them."

"I didn't realize this town had a doctor!"

He nodded, grinning. "We were on the best wagon train. We had a doctor, a minister, a blacksmith, and wonderful cooks with us. All of us pretty much settled together, so it's easy to build the town around the core people we need so much."

"Was everyone here part of your company on the Trail?"

"Not everyone. Fiona's father married a woman from the first wagon train to come through here last year. Melody was on the same train. It's really nice to have new marriage prospects coming through town all the time."

"I can see that it would be," Abby replied. "I'm glad new people are coming in as well. This town is really going to grow."

"Not too big, I hope," Bastian said. "I like this small town the way it is."

She smiled and nodded. "I do too. I'm glad you were the one who traded for me," she said.

"If you make me an apple pie soon, I'll find your father and make him take two more oxen for you. You're a fifteen oxen bride. No doubt in my mind."

She laughed softly. He was hung up on how many oxen she was worth, and she wasn't about to argue with him.

She finished the dishes in silence, knowing he was reading his book. Most men she'd known didn't think they should spend their evenings reading anything, but Bastian was different. She could see why maybe some of the women in town didn't think much of him, but he seemed like a good man to her. Despite his idiosyncrasies, she knew she'd soon be in love with him. Part of her heart was already his.

As soon as the dishes were finished, she looked at him. "We still have an hour or two of daylight. We should go pick apples now."

He didn't have to be asked twice. Bastian was on his feet in an instant. "You get the baskets, and I'll hitch up the wagon."

On the drive to where Fiona had told her the apples were, Abby asked Bastian what they'd done at work that day.

"Oh, we got jars for Emma and the stove for you. Once everything was where it should be we started building an enclosure for the turkeys. I wish we could stick them in with the chickens, but from what I've been told, it's not safe to do that. So, the turkeys will get their own building and fenced yard, just like the chickens. As soon as it's built, I'm going to start working on tracking some turkeys for you. We only need two to start a flock."

"Do you know how to build a trap that will work for them?" she asked.

"Never tried it, but most things I set my mind to doing get done."

She loved the idea of having her turkeys all together ready for her to raise them. "Who takes care of the chickens?" she asked.

"Emma. Her mother is a bit of a chicken expert, so she works with the chickens. I do the hogs. Fiona brought in the goats."

"What about Melody?"

"She had a baby before she could pick an animal. I think she's too enthralled with her baby to really care about raising any animals. I could see her with bunnies though. I'm not sure if she'd have the heart to make them into a pie, though."

Abby's lips twitched. "You really do want some pie, don't you?"

"There's no other reason I would spend a Saturday night out picking apples," he said, turning onto the land where the apples filled the trees. "This isn't anyone's land, so we're just going to pick them."

They each took a basket and picked all the apples they could. "Do you like apple butter?" she asked.

He shrugged. "It's all right. I like apple pies better."

"Of course, you do," she said, grinning. "What about cobbler? Do you like cobbler?"

He nodded emphatically. "Love cobbler. It's almost like pie, but not exactly."

"Cake?" she asked.

He shrugged. "I like all sweets, but pie is my very favorite. I think everyone should have pie at least twice a week."

Abby hated making pie crusts, but she didn't complain. She would be happy to serve him in any way she could.

Once both baskets were full, he asked if it was enough for a pie. "This is enough for a few pies," she said. "But more would be better. Do you think Emma would come out here with me on Monday to pick more?"

"Ask her," he said. He didn't know or care what Emma wanted to do. She had cooked a terrible meal for him once, and he didn't trust her much since then. It had been a joke, but it had been bad enough he'd thought he'd die after eating it.

"I'll ask her at church tomorrow then," she said. "Do you not like Emma?"

"Emma's all right. She's not a great cook though. Not like you and Henri and Fiona and Melody."

"She made lunch for all of us today, and it was delicious," Abby said, glancing at him and trying to understand.

"Henri had to teach her to cook. If we have a church social, make sure you don't get Mrs. Williams's food. She can only make jerky and is a terrible cook otherwise."

"I'll keep that in mind." From his words, she had to surmise that Mrs. Williams was Emma's mother.

That night when they went to bed together, it was much more pleasant for Abby. Bastian took his time with her, and they both enjoyed themselves. He held her for a moment, reminding her that he didn't like to be touched while sleeping.

"That's all right," she said to reassure him. Life with Sebastian was good. Maybe it wasn't what she'd dreamed marriage would be, but it wasn't terrible either. She now had her husband and a new family, and she knew things would only improve.

Chapter Five

Abby woke up excited the following morning. She rinsed the salt off the pork and started a low fire in her new stove. Adding some water, potatoes and carrots, she decided to make the pork as a roast.

Once everything was started, she mixed the dough for bread before rolling out a pie crust. She'd make an apple pie for dessert. She knew her friend would be happy to have food that she didn't have to cook and wasn't prepared over a campfire.

By the time Bastian was awake, she already had the pie put together and ready to go in the oven. "I'm going to do the milking," he said, leaving the house without so much as a good morning.

She shook her head. Her Bastian was full of idiosyncrasies, but he was a good man.

He came back with eggs and milk, looking at her. "What are you doing?" he asked.

"I have our Sunday dinner in the oven. Why?"

He frowned. "I think you skipped a meal."

She laughed. "I'm about to start breakfast. Would you rather have pancakes, johnny cakes or eggs?"

"Eggs and toast, please."

Abby nodded, and immediately started slicing what was left of the loaf of bread they'd had with supper the night before. She was making three loaves that day because she had a little bit more time on her hands. She really did need to see how much laundry needed to be washed. Monday was her preferred wash day. It had always been the day her mother did it, and it seemed to work out.

Once the toast was in the oven, she added a bit of the butter Henri had given her and waited for it to melt. "Scrambled eggs all right?" she asked.

"No, I don't like scrambled. I like mine with all the white done but the yolk runny."

"Will do," she said. She preferred her eggs the same way. She only wished she had bacon to go with the meal. She had already learned that Bastian thought there should be meat and potatoes with every meal. There was just no time to make hash browns because Bastian was hungry.

It didn't take long before the food was on the table. Bastian looked down at his eggs and poked them with a fork before he was satisfied they were done the way he wanted.

After the meal, she cleaned the kitchen. "What time does church start?" she asked.

"Ten. I like to leave about ten minutes before."

She frowned. "You don't socialize before church?"

He shook his head adamantly. "All those voices in that room. It makes me want to stick my fingers in my ears and run away screaming."

"I see." But she didn't. Who would feel that way about being with other followers of Christ? "Can we go a little earlier so I can talk to my friend about coming for Sunday dinner? I don't want to miss having her over because we arrived too late. Maybe you could wait in the wagon for those few minutes."

"I guess that's all right." He really didn't understand why she had to be early, but he'd accommodate her. This once.

"Thank you. I really appreciate it."

She glanced at the clock and saw that it was only eight. She didn't want to wait to see Anna. "Why don't I walk down to the campsite and ask Anna and her husband for dinner, and I'll meet you at the church? That way you can go when you want to."

He frowned. "Why don't you want to go to church with me?"

"I do! Don't think that. I only have a couple more hours I can spend with my friend before she disappears forever."

"I'll drive you down," he said. He really didn't want her to be around her father without him being there. He was afraid the older man would hurt her. Of course, she was smart enough to avoid her father, but he felt safer being with her.

He went out and hitched up the wagon, and she changed into her best dress, which wasn't at all fancy but practical. It would be nice to have something prettier, but she'd already gotten a new stove. She wouldn't be asking for anything else for a good long while.

When he came back inside, he also changed into his Sunday best. He wasn't wearing a suit but wore a nice pair of black slacks, a clean white shirt, a vest, and a tie. He topped off the look with a black cowboy hat. In her eyes he looked incredibly handsome.

"Are you ready?" he asked.

"I am."

"Do you plan to go straight to church from the campsite?"

"I do, if that's all right with you."

"I'm just along for the ride," he said.

As he drove down the hill and to the campsite, he talked nonstop about what he'd read in his horse training book. He talked about how he'd be able to incorporate it into his business. "I need to convince Pa that I should be allowed to work with horses all day instead of helping mend fences." He shook his head. "When we drive the cattle to market next month, I want to stay home."

"You don't think he'll let you?"

Bastian shrugged. "He thinks we must spend all our time building the cattle ranch. Then we can work on our other projects. I disagree. So many out here don't even have a horse and use oxen instead. They would be thrilled to get a trained horse in trade or even pay for it."

"Maybe you could spend your Sundays off working with horses. I'd be happy to help."

He glanced at her and laughed. "A little thing like you? You couldn't help me."

Abby frowned. "I believe I could."

He stopped the wagon outside the circle of wagons the company had made. "Go talk to your friend."

"You should come as well!" she said. "Her husband is a nice man."

Bastian could tell it was important to her, so he got down and helped her to the ground. "Let's go."

Together they made their way through the circle of wagons to where her friend and Steven were. Anna's whole face lit up. "I was hoping I'd get to see you today!"

Abby nodded. "When I heard you were staying here one more day, I thought I'd invite you to Sunday dinner. I already have it in the oven."

Anna looked at Steven, who nodded. "We'd be honored!"

Abby smiled. "Steven, this is my husband, Bastian. Bastian, this is Anna and Steven. Anna has been my best friend since before either of us could walk. We lived next door to each other, and our mothers were good friends."

Bastian nodded. "Nice to meet you both."

Abby noticed he didn't really look at the others, instead focusing on something behind them. "Bastian and his father and brothers own a large ranch together. Bastian is studying and learning all he can about horse training. He wants to breed horses once the ranch is established."

Anna smiled. "How long has your family been here, Bastian?"

"Since 1851. We settled here in October, so a little less than two years. We love it here. The winters are hard, but the summers are cooler." He shrugged. "It's a good place to start over."

Steven nodded. "Do you know if there are any plots left near here?"

"Oh, sure. There are lots. You'd be on the outskirts of the settlement but close enough to shop here and attend our church."

Steven smiled at Anna. "I think we'll be back in the spring then."

"What are you going to do over the winter?" Bastian asked. "We deliberately left earlier than we probably should have so we could settle before winter set in."

Steven shrugged. "We have a bit of money saved up. We'll rent a house or live in a boarding house, whatever we can find. But we'll be back in the spring, and my Anna can have her best friend close by."

Bastian nodded. "Sounds like a good plan. Do you intend to ranch?"

Steven shook his head. "I plan to farm. Crops not animals. We'll have a cow or two for milk, but that's it."

Anna looked over Abby's shoulder. "Your pa is coming this way."

Abby sighed. "Pretend you don't see him."

But her pa walked straight over and glared at his daughter. "He's ready to trade you back, isn't he? Well, I'm not giving up my oxen. I don't need to be burdened with the likes of you."

He pulled back his hand to hit her, but Bastian caught his wrist. "You will not hit my wife."

Pa looked at Bastian curiously. "You're keeping her?"

"This woman is worth at least fifteen oxen, so I know I got the better part of the deal. You will never hit her again; if I have my way, you will never see her again. You are evil, thinking that hitting and kicking your daughter is all right."

"I don't know what lies she told you..."

Bastian frowned. "There were no lies. She has barely mentioned you. I'm speaking from what I've personally seen you try to do."

Her father turned away in disgust. "She needs a firm hand or she'll go wild on you. No one wants a wild wife."

"I think we're going to be all right, but thank you, Mr. Lund."

Her father stomped back to his lonely campsite, where he appeared to be trying to cook a meal for himself. "Excuse me," Abby said, following her father. "What can I make you to eat, Pa?"

Her father glared at her. "I haven't eaten since you left me here to rot."

"I understand. I could put a couple of potatoes on the fire, and you could have baked potatoes after church. They'd go well with some of the jerky."

"Or you could invite me to eat with you and your husband."

Abby shook her head. "No, I couldn't. Bastian would never allow you in our cabin." She felt a rush of emotion for her husband, knowing what she said was true. Bastian could see her father's true nature, and he would never want the man anywhere near her.

Her father frowned. "Fine. Baked potatoes and jerky work."

"Let me show you how to make the potatoes," she said. She knew her father had picked up some potatoes at the mercantile in town, and she was happy to teach him to do for himself.

Bastian walked over and stood beside her watching everything she did. She showed him how to scrub the dirt off the potatoes, make several punctures, and then bury them in the ashes of the fire. "They'll take about forty minutes, but you want to turn them every ten minutes or so. They'll cook evenly that way."

Her pa nodded. "All right."

"I'm sure I could get Anna to fix extra food for you if you contributed to her food supply."

Pa looked at her. "Why would you do that for me?"

"You're my pa," she said.

"Then do it. It will be nice not to have to try to find meals for myself."

"I'll talk to her."

She got to her feet and smiled at Bastian, walking back toward Anna and Steven's wagon. As they walked, Bastian asked, "Why did you help him?"

She shrugged. "I promised my ma I'd take care of him as best I could before he died. I don't see any reason to let him go hungry simply because I'm not finishing the journey."

"You're a good woman," Bastian said. "You're worth at least twenty oxen."

She smiled at him, enjoying how much he thought of her. He improved her worth daily, and that meant she was doing something right.

Back at Anna and Steven's camp, Abby asked her friend about cooking for her father. "He'll provide the food."

Anna sighed. "I can just make enough for one more. He's a better hunter than my Steven, so it'll be fine."

"Thank you," Abby said, hugging her friend. "I feel like I should be taking care of him even if he did trade me for six oxen."

"It should have been twenty," Bastian said again.

Anna laughed. "I think you're right, Bastian. At least twenty."

"I'm not offering him more though. He's mean to my Abby."

Abby's heart fluttered when he called her his. She didn't know why it felt so important that he did so, but she couldn't change how she felt.

Anna frowned for a moment. "It's time to head to the church."

"Ride with us," Abby said. "You'll want a ride up the hill as well, though, we've walked over much worse."

Anna smiled. "But only when we had to."

The four of them headed for the church. When they arrived, Bastian helped Abby down but then stood where he was. "Get a pew and leave the spot on the aisle for me. I'll be in when I hear the music start."

Abby nodded, standing on tiptoe to kiss his cheek. Despite his oddities, he was a good husband to her, and she didn't want him to be uncomfortable.

Anna and Abby found a pew toward the back of the church, and they sat together, leaving the spot on the aisle for Bastian. People swarmed them, coming over to introduce themselves. They all seemed excited to have a new member of the community. When she told people she'd married Bastian, a few had smirked, but she didn't care. What did it matter if he was different? He was good to her.

The sermon that day was on treating all those around you with kindness. "If we're kind to others, and show them how we want to be treated, we'll have a much better chance of receiving kindness in return."

Bastian looked at Abby and nodded. She was certain she understood his thoughts. She'd been kind to a man who had never shown her kindness, but she'd demonstrated how she wanted to be treated.

As they left the church, he said, "I wanted to point to you when the pastor said we should treat others how we want to be treated because you already do that."

Abby smiled, taking his arm. "Thank you for thinking that's how I am. You showed me kindness before I ever showed any to you."

He thought about it for a moment. "I suppose that's true." He helped her into the wagon, and they waited there for the other couple. Abby knew it was going to be a good day. She couldn't wait until Anna and Steven were back in the valley with them, but she'd cling to her husband and his wonderful family for now.

She couldn't quite believe how fortunate she'd been to find someone who knew how to care for others.

It didn't matter how her father felt about her or what she was leaving behind as she moved to this new community. She planned to be happy and that was that.

Chapter Six

As soon as they got home, Abby rushed inside to put the bread and the pie in the oven. They'd have to wait a little bit to eat, but knowing how food was on the trail, Abby was certain there would be no complaints.

While Anna and Abby chatted, Bastian took Steven out to see the horses. "I plan on getting them all trained as soon as I can. When you come back in the spring, we may have to talk about horses."

Steven nodded. "I'd come to you first," he said. "I'm glad Abby is with you. I've known her and Anna since we were all small children, and it's good to see Abby with a man who isn't abusive."

Bastian shook his head. "That man is evil. I would have traded for Abby even if I hadn't been interested in her as a wife. I'd have found her a job or something. The way that man treated her turns my stomach. And she helped him today."

"Abby has a strong sense of responsibility. She took care of her sick mother for a good portion of the trip. She was always the one to cook and do laundry for her family, and her father treated her as if she was lower than a servant. It made me angry, but Anna kept telling me not to interfere, so I didn't."

"I don't think it would have done any good. I didn't think she should help him today, but she explained she'd promised her mother she'd look out for him as best she could. And that was part of that promise."

Steven nodded, his eyes on one of the foals in the stable. "I want the one with the white stripe on his nose."

Bastian nodded. "I call him skunk. Do you want to ride him, or do you want him as part of a team?"

"Could he pull a buggy on his own? I'm hoping I can have a single horse to pull my wife."

Bastian nodded. "He'll be able to when he's grown." He pointed to another horse. "That stallion is his sire, and that mare is his mother. I think he'll be one of the strongest horses coming out of this stable."

"Sounds good to me. Skunk is my horse of choice then."

"I'll make sure to have him ready in the spring."

In the cabin, Abby and Anna chatted as if they could never talk to one another again. "Do you think Steven really will select a parcel of land in this area?" Abby asked. "I so want you to move close!"

Anna nodded. "He knows he'll have a very weepy wife on his hands if he doesn't, and he hates it when I cry."

"I hate it when you cry too!"

Anna carried the roast pork to the table while Abby whipped up gravy to go with their meal. "This feels like a feast after so long on the trail," Anna said. "And you seem to have settled right into your new life."

"I have the most amazing mother and sisters-in-law. They treat me as if I've been around forever. We all share housework every day. Lately we've been canning different vegetables, but I've convinced Emma, one of my sisters-in-law, to pick apples with me tomorrow. I'm hoping we can find enough for me to make pies on for months. Apparently, my dear husband is obsessed with pie."

Anna grinned. "You shouldn't have a hard time making him happy then. You've always made the best pies!"

"I hate making them," Abby confessed.

"Who doesn't? Pie crusts are a pain, but I'm sure he appreciates your efforts."

"We'll have apple pie for lunch today. I added a bit more cinnamon than usual because I think it will taste better that way. But you'll tell me exactly what you think of the pie, right?"

"Always have and always will," Anna responded. "So, how are things in the bedroom?"

Abby looked at her in shock. "You can't ask me that!"

"You're my best friend. If I can't ask you that, I can't ask anyone."

"Things are fine. Last night was much better than the night before."

"Every night will be better," Anna said. "I find myself thinking about our lovemaking throughout the day, and I can't wait for him to hold me at night. My first couple of nights with Steven were really bad, but it got better with time. Now I even initiate lovemaking sometimes."

Abby frowned. "I'm not sure I could ever do that!"

"Sure, you could. You've always been strong and outspoken."

"I guess I have..."

Anna went to the window and looked out. "It looks like the men are headed back to the house."

"Good." Abby pulled the pie out of the oven and set it on the worktable to cool. Then she removed the bread, carrying two loves to the table and leaving one beside the pie. She put the little butter she had left onto the table with everything else, and then she sat down at the foot of the table while they waited for the men to come inside.

A moment later, Bastian and Steven were inside, and they took seats at the table with Bastian sitting across from Abby, and Anna across from Steven. "I really like the cabin," Anna said to Bastian.

He shrugged. "Keeps us warm in winter."

"I'm sure it does."

Bastian lowered his head and said a quick prayer over their meal. Abby was happy to share their food with the others. It made her feel good to do something nice for her friend who had always watched out for her.

While they ate, they talked about how nice it would be if Steven and Anna moved to Clover Creek. "I hate that you still have so much travel to do before you can claim your land," Abby said.

Steven nodded. "I'm half tempted to leave Anna with you, but I'd starve to death, and there wouldn't be anywhere for her to live. I hate that she must endure the hardship with me."

Bastian shrugged. "She'll be fine. All my brothers married women who had gone to Oregon and come back."

Anna nodded emphatically. "I wouldn't want to be away from you for six months either. It's hard to do what you need to do when you love someone so much."

Bastian made a face. "If I thought it would be best for Abby to continue on to Oregon City, I'd make sure she did that. I don't think my feelings could matter at all."

"You couldn't send me away from you," Abby protested. "My job is to be here with you."

"I guess it is," Bastian said. "But if it weren't safe, I wouldn't let you stay."

"But you paid six oxen for me!"

"You were worth so much more!"

Abby just laughed. "You keep telling me that."

Anna smiled. "I'm glad someone other than me can see your worth. You're awfully special, Abby."

After they'd eaten, Anna helped with the dishes, and the two women sat and chatted some more. They waited a little while to have the pie, but when Abby served it, she could see how excited Bastian was by it. "Are these the apples we picked last night?" he asked.

Abby nodded. "Yes, I thought you'd appreciate a pie."

"I always love pie," he said. "You should make another for tomorrow night."

"I'm hoping that Emma and I can get a bunch more of those apples, and I can put up pie filling for the winter. Then we can have pies until next spring when more fruits will be in season."

Bastian sighed happily. "You are a twenty-five oxen wife. How could your father undervalue you so much?"

Anna laughed. "I thought she was a twenty oxen wife earlier."

"Oh, she was, but her value went up as soon as I tasted her pie."

"I wish I'd taken the time to whip some cream to go on top, but I'll make sure to do that next time."

Bastian smiled contentedly. "You keep feeding me pie, and I'll keep you forever!"

"I thought you were already planning to keep me forever," Abby countered.

"I guess so. But the pie makes it more realistic."

When it was time to say goodbye to her friend, Abby could feel the tears welling up in her eyes. There had been very few days in her life without Anna beside her, and she was about to have six months of those days at least.

The two friends hugged tearfully, and the men shook hands. "Hurry back," Bastian said, looking at his wife's face. She looked utterly bereft. He'd never had a friend like Anna was to Abby, but he had very strong feelings for his brothers. Perhaps that was the same.

When they were gone, Bastian pulled Abby down on his lap and simply held her while she cried. When she finally sat up straight and wiped her eyes, he said, "I have some crates in the cellar. We could go pick more apples."

"But that's what Emma and I are doing tomorrow. We'll have blackberries this week too. I wonder what apple-blackberry pie would taste like."

Bastian shrugged. "Delicious, I'm sure."

"Do you like jelly? I could make some apple jelly as well. Then you could have jelly for your toast."

He shrugged. "I like it all right, but I really prefer pie."

"Pie it is." She'd make sure to get a jar or two of apple jelly for herself, but he obviously would rather she made pie filling out of every apple they picked. "I'll also do our laundry tomorrow. I'll probably wash right after breakfast so I can still pick apples early."

He nodded. "All my dirty clothes are in the loft."

"The loft?" she asked. That made no sense. Why would he climb up there to store his dirty clothes.

He nodded. "You can just go up there and throw them over the edge, then you can take them out and wash them. Do you need anything from me?"

Abby shook her head, though she still wondered why he'd put his dirty clothes in the loft where they were harder to reach.

She got her answer the following morning as she and Emma were driving out to pick apples, planning to fill the crates Bastian had provided. "Do you have any idea why Bastian would put his dirty clothes in the loft?"

Emma sighed. "He throws them up there after they are too dirty to keep wearing. It keeps them out of the way, and he doesn't have to think about them, until one of us tells him we're going to do laundry."

Abby wanted to ask why he did it that way, but she was afraid of the answer. Bastian did some things in a way that seemed so illogical to her that she wondered how they'd ever get along.

While picking the apples, Emma and Abby got to know one another better. "How did it come about that you and your brother married brother and sister?"

Emma shrugged. "Henri had her eye on Roy before we left Independence the same way I had my eye on Jared. By the time we got here, our crushes had been in our minds for a long time. It turned out Jared had been eyeing me, and Roy had been eyeing Henri. We were married soon after we settled here, and the weddings were only a week apart."

"Bastian said something about not trusting your cooking?"

Emma blushed. "I had no idea what a terrible cook my mother was until after I'd gotten to know Henri and her family. I made supper one night for the Applebys, and it was a burnt mess. I thought it was delicious, and I expected praise. Instead, we ended up eating the meal

Henri had left in the kitchen. Jared tried to tell the others it was a joke that I'd made such a terrible meal, but I don't think anyone believed it. Before he'd marry me, Jared made me agree to get cooking lessons from Henri, which is why the two of us are so close."

"I love your cooking!" Abby said.

"That's because Henri spent months and months training me on how to be a better cook. I had never made a loaf of bread before I met Henri. My mother fried rice up in a pan with no water, and we all thought it was supposed to be crunchy." Emma shook her head. "Ma's learned a lot from Henri as well, but lots of things she still cooks her own way. My family celebrates when Henri invites them over for meals."

Abby smiled. "And are you and Roy the only two in your family?"

"No. I have two younger sisters. I'm surprised they weren't down at the campsite trying to find men they could be happy with. They both want to marry, but they're young."

"It must be nice to have sisters."

"Sometimes. Do you have any siblings?" Emma asked.

Abby shook her head. "No, Ma had only me. Pa wanted a son, something fierce, but it never worked out that way. It was always just me. I think that's part of why he wanted to trade me. He would have preferred to take a son, but oxen were the only thing offered."

"Jared told me that every day Bastian says you are worth more oxen than the last. Is it strange for him to keep talking about that?"

"Sure," Abby said, "but Bastian seems just a bit odd, so I don't worry about it too much."

Emma nodded. "Bastian is a good man, but you're right. There's just something different about him. He's smart as a whip, and he's kind, but he doesn't seem to understand other people very well."

"You're right. He doesn't."

By noon, the two women had filled six crates with apples. Abby had even climbed one of the trees and dropped apples to Emma who stood with her apron held out in front of her.

"What are we doing with all these apples?" Emma asked. "There's no way we can eat them all before they rot."

"We're making apple pie filling. Bastian seems to be a bit obsessed with pie."

Emma laughed. "I hope you plan to share with all the families."

"Of course, I do! I want to do the same with blackberries. Perhaps by the end of the harvest, I'll have enough pie filling put up to make enough pies to keep Bastian happy through the whole winter."

"I hope you do. We all love pie!"

"Are there any other berries or anything we can pick?"

Emma thought for a moment. "Chokecherries! They're ripe now, and we can pick them. The trees usually grow in stream beds. I bet we could go pick some tomorrow. And we'll do blackberries on Wednesday. Then Thursday, Friday, and Saturday we'll make jams, jellies, and pie filling."

"I've never had chokecherries, but I'll figure out how to make them into pie filling."

"Plan to pick as many as possible tomorrow then." Emma smiled. "It's nice to have someone who isn't expecting to harvest with."

Abby grinned. "I do hope to have a baby before too terribly long, but I'm glad I can be your harvest friend for now."

"Harvest sister," Emma said. "Now, we're harvest sisters."

Chapter Seven

That week was full of activity with harvesting a great deal more of the garden and Abby and Emma's little excursions to find more pie ingredients and picking them as well.

Saturday night, Abby made a pot pie from some of the beef Melody had given her. When Bastian walked in the door, he immediately identified the smell as pie crust. "What are you making?" he asked.

"Beef pie. And a surprise." She hadn't told him about the chokecherries she and Emma had harvested, wanting to surprise him with a sweet treat.

"As long as I get pie, I'm happy. But I'll take any surprise you want to give me." He washed his hands then sat at the table, waiting patiently for his meal.

Abby couldn't help but smile. He never greeted her with a kiss, but he made it clear what was important to him. Marriage to Bastian was quite different than what she'd imagined it would be, but it was a good life.

She served dinner and filled their cups with milk. As soon as she joined him at the table, he bowed his head to pray, obviously too excited about the pie to wait another minute.

When he took his first bite of the pie, he closed his eyes, savoring the taste. "This is amazing," he said after chewing his food.

"I'm so glad you like it! Henri offered me her receipt for it, but I decided to use the one my ma always made."

Bastian nodded. "I'd rarely say there is something out there better than Henri's cooking, but this is. Tell her to keep her receipts to herself!"

Abby laughed, taking a bite herself. Henri was a wonderful cook, and if he thought she was better at any meal than Henri, she'd take it as a compliment.

As soon as they were finished with their meal, she asked, "Do you want your surprise now? Or later?"

"Now, of course. I have no patience to wait for anything that I may like."

Abby laughed. "I'll go get it then." First, she carried two small plates to the table, then she went back for forks and the pie.

When she put it on the table, he looked at it for a moment. "That's not apple or blackberry."

"We found some ripe chokecherry."

He winced. "Chokecherries are so sour!"

"I think you'll like what I did with them," she said. "I sweetened them up but left just a bit of their tartness."

"I'll try it, but no promises that I'll like it."

"I sure hope you do. We canned sixty jars of the pie filling and another twenty of the jelly. We all tried it and liked the end results."

She watched him closely as he took his first bite. "Oh, that's actually good!"

"I'm so glad! It took more sugar than I wanted to part with, but I think having enough for a pie a month for a year was worth it. We have blackberry and apple pie filling done as well."

He smiled. "Fabulous!"

"And the ladies gave me some of the raspberry pie filling they did early in the year. And strawberries, of course. We should have a pie-filled winter. They said the cherries and currants weren't great this year, but we'll go pick those in the spring as well. So many pies!"

Bastian took another bite of his pie with a big smile on his face. "I love that we have such a variety here."

"They said next summer we'll try to get some huckleberries as well. They said they only grow high in the mountains, so we may have to spend a night in the mountains getting them before we return home."

He frowned. "I don't like the idea of that. You could reach the mountains across the valley and pick huckleberries there. It should only take a couple of hours to get there, then you can pick for a few hours and drive back. I don't want you to have to spend another night away from me."

She smiled. It was the most emotion for her he'd ever shared. Sure, they'd only been married for a week, but they were planning to spend their entire lives together.

She pursed her lips for a moment, wanting to bring up a new topic. "Henri told me there's going to be a church social next weekend, and there will be dancing. Can we go?"

He frowned for a moment before nodding slowly. "I'll stay as long as I can. Sometimes the music gets too loud and the people stomping on the floor becomes too much for me, and I have to leave."

She nodded, wishing there was a way to help him through the experience. She could say she didn't want to go, but it would be a lie. She loved to dance. "We can leave as soon as it becomes too much for you." She covered his hand with hers. "Thank you for being willing to go even though it's outside your comfort."

"You're worth it," he said softly. "I think your father should have received thirty oxen for you. No one has ever been able to make chokecherries into something I could eat, and here I am, enjoying every bite of this pie. You're something special."

She shook her head. "You bring out the best in the people around you."

He looked skeptical at that but didn't argue with her. "I talked to my pa about the foal Steven wants today."

"What did he say?" Abby asked. She hoped he could train the foal and stay home from the cattle drive.

"Pa said I could stay home and work on training it. He said someone should stay home and make sure the ranch didn't fall apart while they were gone." Bastian looked excited. He only seemed so happy when he was talking about training horses or eating pie.

"That's wonderful!"

Bastian nodded. "He wants us to stay in the big house with Melody as well. He thinks it will be better if we're there with her."

"All right." Abby didn't care where they stayed as long as Bastian was allowed to train Skunk. "Emma and Fiona are going to stay together as well. Probably in Emma's house because she has a real house and not just a cabin."

"I need to read up on how to start the training with a foal. I've mostly read about breaking wild horses, but that won't be necessary with Skunk."

She smiled, understanding that was her cue to do the dishes. "You read, and I'll deal with cleaning up."

While she washed the dishes, she thought about how very basic Bastian's interactions always were. There was never a need to ask him what he was thinking because he tended to blurt it out as he went about his business. Often, she heard him having entire conversations with himself, usually about horse training, but once she'd heard him ranking his favorite pies in order.

She finished the dishes and sat down at the table, pulling a book of her own toward her. Fiona had loaned it to her, and she was thrilled to have a story to read. Bastian would be too involved in his studies to really talk to her.

As she was getting ready for bed that evening, she thought again about what a good man she'd married. He may never love her as much as pie, but he made her life as good as he possibly could.

Church was interesting the following day. There was another group of emigrants camped there, and Abby enjoyed meeting them, though the whole time she was being introduced, she was thankful she wasn't continuing her journey west.

One young man seemed to have his eye on Roy and Emma's younger sister, Abigail, who was called Victoria or Vicki, by everyone but family, who insisted on using her middle name. Abby was relieved she could call the girl Vicki instead of by her own name. That would just be odd in her opinion.

After watching Vicki and the young man talk for a long while, Abby walked over to be introduced. Vicki smiled at her. "This is Abby, and she married my sister-in-law's brother who is also my sister's brother-in-law. Our families ended up mingling a little."

The man smiled. "It's nice to meet you, Abby. I'm John."

"So good to meet you, John. I hope you'll be settling around this area."

John looked at Vicki as he said, "I'll be settling here. My parents don't know where they want to go, but I know this is the place for me."

Vicki blushed. "I'll look forward to seeing you in the spring then."

Abby smiled, moving away. She felt as if she'd done all she could for Vicki's love life. When she glanced back, she noticed Bastian was gone. She tried not to linger too long after he'd had to leave the church.

She followed him outside and stood beside him, letting him know she was ready to leave whenever he was. "The emigrants seem nice. One of them has his eye on Vicki."

Bastian sighed. "She's too young to marry."

"From what I understand, she's the same age Emma was when she married Jared."

"That's different," Bastian said.

"Why?"

"Just is."

Abby decided not to continue to argue with him. He was being stubborn. "Are we still going for a picnic down by the lake today?" she asked. "I packed a lunch for us, and there's a blanket to eat on."

He frowned for a moment and then nodded. "I forgot we'd talked about that. Yes, we'll go, and I'll wait and start Skunk's training until I've studied just a bit more."

Abby bit her lip. "If you want to train Skunk, we can have a picnic another day." Though she was sure it would have to be in the spring if they put it off. The weather was already getting nippy.

He shook his head. "I'd forgotten, but I never don't follow through on a promise."

"All right. The picnic basket and blanket are in the back of the wagon."

He walked to the wagon, helped her up, and then they started their long drive to Bear Lake. She hadn't had the opportunity to see it yet, and she was excited.

As they drove, she questioned Bastian about what he'd learned about training foals. She could have chosen any topic, but she knew Bastian would have worked it around to talking about training foals anyway.

When they reached the lake, Abby was thrilled. "It's huge!" she said. "And I love how the mountains appear behind it. It just makes me want to jump right in."

He chuckled. "I don't think that's a great idea. Though I know there were a group of young men who thought it would be funny to take the plunge in January. Out of the ten men who jumped in, only one died. That's not bad considering how cold it was."

Abby shook her head. "That doesn't sound very smart to me."

"It wasn't!" he told her. "The others were sick. Two caught pneumonia."

"I'm glad you were smart enough not to go with them."

Bastian sighed. "I try to be logical about everything."

She spread the blanket and spread out the food she'd made. "Do you want me to fix your plate?"

He shook his head. "No, I'll take what I want."

"I did bring what was left of our pie from last night."

He grinned at her. "You know, you are the best wife a man like me could have asked for."

"I want to be worth those six oxen," she said.

"You're worth at least thirty-five. Any woman who can make chokecherries taste like something I'd want to eat daily is worth more than six." He sat on the blanket and chose the foods he wanted. She was a bit disappointed when he skipped over the green beans.

"What vegetables do you like?" she asked.

"Potatoes, peas, carrots, and onion if it's cooked really well through."

"And that's all?" she asked. It was best to know. If she could only fix those vegetables for the rest of her life, then that's what she'd do.

Bastian nodded. "The others all feel weird in my mouth. I don't know why, but I can't force myself to eat them."

"That's fine. If I want other vegetables, we'll eat them for lunch," she said.

While they ate, she stared out at the water. It seemed quiet, with little movement, and there didn't seem to be even one boat out on it. "Do you go out on boats during the summer?" she asked.

Bastian shrugged. "There's really no time for frivolities during the summer. Or any other time of year. Being a rancher is hard work, and if I want to have the right to train horses, I need to do my share plus some."

"I see," Abby said, though she wished things were different. Her father had been the same way, never willing to do anything but work. "What do you do when you have a minute or two for fun?"

He shrugged. "I usually just read about horse training."

"All right. I should make sure I always have a book on hand then so we can read together."

He nodded, not seeming terribly interested. "Did you know if you blow on a horse's nose, they will learn your scent and be more likely to do what you need them to do when you train them?"

She smiled. "Is that so?"

While they finished their meal, he talked to her about different methods of horse training, and she listened with a smile. He couldn't seem to focus on more than one thing at a time, but that was all right with her. It was nice to listen to his voice sometimes. And she'd never met a man who wasn't looking for a good conversationalist. She'd never have to worry about trying to find topics to talk to Sebastian about. He'd just change the topic to what he wanted to talk about anyway.

On the drive home, she daydreamed as he reiterated everything he'd told her during their picnic. She couldn't help imagining a little boy who became as focused on one thing as his father. She could imagine her son saying, "Mama, I found a new kind of dung today. I know it's not cow or horse, but now I need to find out what kind of dung it is. Do you think you could help?"

Chapter Eight

Abby spent the following week harvesting the garden and putting up all they could with the other women in the family. All of them had worked together on the garden, so they all worked together to can the produce and shared it among them. At times, Vicki and Barbara, Emma's other sister, joined them.

Both girls would pay very close attention to anything cooked, and they'd taken over many cooking days from their mother, now that they had learned what food should taste like.

Saturday, they finished early so they could all go to their respective homes and make a dish for the church social. "Many families can't afford to take a meat dish, so those of us that can, usually do. It makes things easier for all," Henri said as they separated.

"I was planning to make a chicken pie," Abby said. "Will that work?"

"Absolutely!" Henri said. "Though you may want to make two or three. Everyone is supposed to take enough to feed their entire family, but when the food is scarce, it's easier if some of the families make more."

Abby nodded. "I'll make three then. I know it won't disappoint Bastian."

Henri nodded, laughing. "He got mad at Ma and me if we made cookies or cake. He always just wanted pie."

"I've noticed that about him. I've made three pies this week, and every time he finds me after eating the last piece and gives me this sad look as he tells me the pie is all gone. It's like he hasn't quite connected the fact that once he's eating a slice, there will be one less slice to look forward to."

Henri grinned. "That's my Bastian!"

"I think he's mine now," Abby said.

"You can keep him then!" Henri said with a laugh and a wave, as she carried the baby down the hill to her own cabin.

Abby smiled as she hurried into the cabin to roll out four pie crusts. She had to make three for the social, but he'd also want a fruit pie. She reached for the raspberry pie filling and set it aside, ready to put it into the pie crust once it was ready.

She dressed in her Sunday best after the pies were in the oven, and she carefully put her hair into a bun appropriate for a married lady. She'd always worn braids up until then, but it didn't seem at all dignified for a married woman to wear braids.

The pies were cooling by the time Bastian got in from working with his father and brothers. He hurried and changed, wearing his Sunday best as well. Abby knew she needed to make a few dresses for herself, but there would be no time until after the harvest, and she'd ask for fabric then.

When Bastian was ready, he looked at Abby. "You ready to go?"

She nodded. "Just remember to tell me when it gets too loud, and we can leave."

He nodded. "I may have to step outside to eat, but if I do, I'll come back to you when I'm done."

He helped her carry the pies out to the wagon, and they stowed them in a couple of crates. No one wanted a squashed pie!

When they got to the church, she saw that the yard was even busier than it usually was on Sundays, but then she realized there was another company camping. She'd been told this would be the last one for the year, which was good. It was already frosting in the mornings.

She joined the other ladies in the church, who had set up a line for food. She stood behind her pot pies and was ready to serve them, but she'd left the sweet pie at home, knowing that Bastian wouldn't want to share it.

As the men slowly came through the line, asking for the different things they wanted, she noted that most of the people from the camp must be there, but there were no women she didn't recognize in line.

They must be serving the people from the wagon train, and she thought that was delightful. An entire community was willing to share their food with the emigrants who were walking through their town in search of freedom in the West. She knew her entire company would have been incredibly grateful for the opportunity to have one meal they didn't have to cook, hunt, or use their own food for, but it hadn't happened. No, this community was something special.

Bastian ignored everyone's food on his way through the line, and only got pot pie from Abby. "I need more," he said when she placed two pieces on his plate. She laughed and gave him a bit more.

"You have to share. We're feeding the camp."

"I know."

She leaned forward and whispered, "There's a sweet pie waiting at home."

He grinned. "I won't ask for more then. I don't know what I did to deserve a wife like you, but I'm sure glad I did it."

All three pies were gone quickly, and when Henri, who was standing beside her, noticed that her food was gone, she said, "Now you get to go and get in line."

"Really? There's plenty more to serve."

"Get in line!"

Abby grinned, removing her apron and walking around the long table to join the back of the line. She chose a little of everything, not wanting to hurt anyone's feelings. Besides, she'd never been picky about food. As long as there was something to eat, she was happy.

She joined a group of women from the company coming through their community, chatting easily with them. "I'm glad you guys came when you did. This is the first church social we've had since I stopped here a couple of weeks ago."

"How did you just stop here?" one of the women asked.

"I met a man here and stayed. We've been married for a couple of weeks," she said, leaving out the fact that her husband had purchased her with oxen. It wasn't something she really wanted to talk about, though she and Bastian joked about it often.

"Oh, how romantic!" a girl who couldn't have been more than sixteen said. "I hope I meet my future husband soon."

Abby smiled. She didn't know the girl, and it was up to the girl's mother if she was allowed to marry so young. "It's a beautiful place and a wonderful group of people here."

"It seems like it," one of the older women said. "You're the first community to allow us to eat with them, and it is much appreciated."

Abby nodded. "I know this never happened when I was on the Trail. We treated a couple of people from my company before they moved on, but I don't recall anyone doing something like this. Makes me proud to be part of something so kind."

"I should think so!"

After their meal, several men from around town moved to one corner of the church and began playing music. Abby tapped her toes, enjoying it, but she joined the other women to wash up after the meal.

When they were finished cleaning, Abby went outside to find Bastian. He was leaning up against their wagon, talking to a stranger. "Do you think we could dance once?"

Bastian nodded. "As long as I come out between dances, and you don't mind coming to get me, I should be able to keep going tonight."

Abby's face lit up. This was her first dance to attend, where she had a man who was hers. It was nice to be able to go out and dance.

The song was a fast one, which didn't seem to bother Bastian one bit. He virtually threw her around the dancefloor, spinning her and bobbing back and forth. When the song was over, he smiled. "Come get me when you're ready."

"I think I'll choose a slower song next time."

Bastian laughed. "You're fun to dance with."

Abby found an empty chair and collapsed into it, and Henri found her quickly. "I can't believe you let him throw you around like that. I've never seen a girl last through a whole song dancing with Bastian."

Abby laughed. "It was fun."

Henri shook her head. "I've always heard there's someone for everyone, but it wasn't until I saw you dance with Bastian that I really believed it. I'm so glad you married my brother."

"I am too," Abby said, grinning. Dancing with Bastian was fun, but she would try a much slower song next time.

They stayed until the men packed up their instruments to go home. Abby wandered outside to find Bastian again talking to someone. "The music is over."

Bastian nodded. "I guess my wife wants to go home, and I want to eat the pie she made me."

The other man laughed. "Have a nice night!"

"You too."

Bastian helped Abby into the wagon and drove home. "I spent the whole night listening to other men complain about their wives. I'm so glad I married a woman who gives me nothing to complain about."

Abby laughed. "I'm sure you'll have complaints about me as time goes on."

Bastian shrugged. "I don't think so. You're the perfect wife for me."

At home, she carried the empty pie plates inside while she put two plates on the table and cut the pie that was waiting for them. She was glad she'd made all three pot pies, because she hadn't realized they were feeding the company camped there. It made it a great deal easier for them to feed everyone when people brought triple what they would feed their own families.

Bastian walked in and washed his hands before finding his spot at the table. "Two pieces please."

Abby laughed. "You earned them by dancing with me."

He grinned. "I'll happily do just about anything for pie."

"I've noticed that about you."

THE MEN WERE LEAVING on Monday to drive the cattle to market. This was their first year to do so, as they'd used the previous year to build up their herds. Even if the winter was difficult, Abby knew they had enough food stored for the winter, especially since they were keeping several steers for the beef.

The women had told her that as soon as they got back from the cattle drive, the men would spend all their time hunting, so they would have wild game to add to their food supplies. Abby had never lived in such an out of the way place, so she was surprised at how little they could count on receiving from the store.

The men would be gone for three weeks and would return home tired and needing homecooked meals from what Henri had said. But while they were gone, it would make chores a little easier on the women.

She would move enough clothes into Melody's house on Monday afternoon that she shouldn't have to go home much when they were gone.

They all woke early on Monday, and the women served a hot breakfast in the main house for the men before they left. Melody seemed concerned, but she tried to cover it up. "I think you should let the younger men go, and you stay home with me," she said to Pa.

He chuckled. "I was only two years younger than I am now when I traveled the Oregon Trail. Surely, I'm still young enough to go to Idaho Falls on a cattle drive."

Melody frowned, but reluctantly nodded. "Make sure you build a good fire every night."

They were taking a trail cook and all but four of the cowboys, leaving a skeleton crew for Bastian and the women. "Hurry, but not too fast," Bastian said. "Go at a fast, safe pace. There're mountain passes that you'll need to take slowly."

The entire meal was spent with advice given and mostly ignored by the men leading the cattle drive. "Maybe next year, you'll feel safe just sending the men," Emma said.

Jared shook his head at his wife. "No, one of us will always need to go. We don't want our men absconding with the cattle."

"Are you worried they will?" Emma asked, surprised.

He laughed. "No, not really. Especially not with so many of us going along with them. The men are used to taking orders from us."

Bastian grinned. "I hope to have that foal eating out of my hand by the time you get back."

"I'm sure that won't be hard for you," Sam said. "You've always had a way with animals."

Bastian nodded. He was excited about the cattle drive because it meant they would finally see a return on their investment, but he really didn't want to go. Especially not with a brand new wife he enjoyed being with.

As the men left, the women stood on the front porch of the big house and waved to them. Bastian was already off and working with Skunk and giving the men staying home their instructions for the day.

There wasn't a dry eye on any of the women. Even Abby shed a tear watching them go, though hers was mostly a sympathy tear for her friends and new sisters.

When they went back into the quiet house, Melody said, "I think we need to harvest everything still in the garden and can it today. Then we won't be thinking about what we're missing."

Abby nodded emphatically. "Emma and I can harvest while the rest of you start the canning process."

Henri smiled. "I'd like that a lot."

Emma and Abby carried their baskets outside and carefully picked everything from the garden. They didn't want to leave a single thing that could be eaten. It would seem wasteful.

It took them most of the first day with just a short break for lunch. When they finally carried the last of the produce inside, Melody told them they were taking the rest of the day off. "You can help us with the canning tomorrow, but you did the bulk of the work by getting all the food out of the garden. Thank you!"

The other women echoed Melody's thanks.

"We'll all have supper together here every night," Melody said. "Many hands make the work so much easier."

Abby smiled, nodding. She was sore from all the harvesting but glad it was done. Now it was just a matter of canning what they could and storing the rest. It had been a hard day of work, but it was worth it.

Chapter Nine

After a couple of days, Abby realized that she really didn't like staying in Melody's house. She loved her mother-in-law and the baby, but she didn't like how strange she felt being in bed with her husband in someone else's home.

She got up early each morning, fixing breakfast for the three of them, but Melody cooked the rest of the meals. And she rarely made pies, which made Bastian sad.

By the end of the three weeks, they had all the crops harvested and canned, and she was happy with their accomplishment, but she was ready to go home and live with just her husband again.

When the men got home, they were dead tired, but his pa had perked up when Bastian asked how it had gone. "We got ten dollars per head more than expected. It was a very profitable trip."

"That's great, Pa!"

His father nodded. "I can see what you're thinking. If we got paid that much more than we thought, we can move you to full-time horse training, and you're right, we can. As soon as I can get two more cowboys working for us, you'll be able to train."

Bastian looked happier than Abby had ever seen him. "That's great!"

Bastian hugged her close, the first time he'd voluntarily shown affection for her in public. Oh, he helped her down from the wagon or helped her up, but other than that, he didn't touch her publicly. It was odd to her, but she didn't complain. A woman worth forty-six oxen—which he'd declared she was just the night before—didn't complain.

As they walked home, she thought about the pie she'd made earlier that day and smiled. They'd been expecting the men to arrive any day, so she'd gone home and made a pie that afternoon, thinking if his brothers and father didn't arrive home, they could take a walk over to the cabin, and she could make sure he got his pie.

She smiled as they walked home after spending a little time with his father and brothers. "I have a surprise for you at home."

"Pie?" he asked. "I can't believe I've gone this long without eating one of your pies. I feel positively lost without it."

She laughed. "Yes, it's pie. I did a mix of blackberry and raspberry for this one."

He grinned. "I can't wait!"

"You don't have to. I baked it earlier today, and it's been cooling all afternoon." They'd finished supper right before the men had driven in, so she didn't need to cook immediately. They just needed to finish their pie and maybe spend some time in bed together. They hadn't made love during the three weeks they'd spent at Melody's house, and she was surprised at how very much she missed it.

She got them each a piece of pie, leaving the rest of it on the table, knowing he'd want more than one or two pieces. "I'm sorry I didn't feel like I could cook pie every day while we were living with Melody, but I wasn't about to suggest we come back here. Melody needed someone there for support."

"It's all right. Just make lots of pies now to make up for it." His entire focus was on his pie, and he had four pieces before he stopped. "Three pieces left for tomorrow. You can have one and I'll have two, unless you don't like this pie, and then I'll eat all three."

She laughed. "You can have all the pie. I don't mind."

He grinned, his teeth interesting colors from the pie. "Have I mentioned what a wonderful wife you are yet today?"

She shook her head. "No, but I'm starting to believe you when you do say it."

"Have I ever mentioned that I wanted to flog your pa?"

"No, I don't believe you have."

"When I saw him raise his boot to kick you, I wanted to hurt him. But he stopped in time that I had no excuse for beating him."

"Thank you for wanting to save me from him."

"I got the best wife I could have asked for as part of the bargain."

She laughed. "You only think that because I make so many pies for you."

"No, you're wonderful in other ways as well." He stretched. "Speaking of which, I think we should go to bed early tonight."

"Oh?" she asked, grinning.

"Yes. It felt lonely sleeping with you at Melody's. You never invited me to play on your side of the bed."

She laughed. "I'll be ready to play just as soon as I finish up these dishes," she said. "How did it go with Skunk today?"

"I think he's turning into a wonderful horse. He lets me put a saddle on him, and he doesn't try to fight me when I lead him by rope. He's going to be a fine horse for Steven and Anna."

"I hope they do come back in the spring," she said. She worried often that her friend and her husband would find a place they liked better between there and Oregon City, and then she'd be left alone without her best friend. She'd made good friends there in Clover Creek, but that didn't mean she didn't miss Anna something fierce.

Bastian looked at her. "You miss her but not your pa."

Abby nodded, even though she felt a bit guilty admitting her feelings. "I do."

"Do you miss your ma?"

"Yes. I miss her a lot. The two of us were very close. If she was around Pa wouldn't even kick me."

Bastian shook his head. "Did he kick you often?"

Abby shrugged, not sure what often meant when it came to kicking fathers. "Dishes are finished," she said, glad to be able to change the topic. She didn't want to think about how her father had treated her. She wanted to think about her bright future with Bastian.

He stood and walked to her, scooping her into his arms and making her laugh. "Bed!"

"I couldn't agree more."

His lovemaking that night was as sweet as honey. He'd learned exactly what she liked and didn't like, and he made sure she was always satisfied before he let himself go. They'd both learned a lot about each other in the month of their marriage.

Afterward, he laid on his side and held her close. "Fifty oxen. That's what I should have paid for you."

She chuckled and snuggled close to him. "However many you want," she said softly.

To her surprise, he forgot about his rule about people touching him while he slept that night. He held her close and never once complained. She felt bereft for a moment when he turned from her in the middle of the night to sleep on his side facing the wall. It had been nice touching for so long.

She quickly drifted back to sleep, dreaming about her wonderful life. It seemed that nothing would stand in the way of her happiness. It was time things finally went her way.

Now that she knew it was his favorite, she woke early and fixed bacon, eggs, and toast for breakfast. When he came in from the milking, he carried a bucket of milk that he set on the work table. "Skunk got so excited when he saw me that he rushed over and nudged me with his nose. I'm going to miss him."

"It won't be profitable if you only train the horses you want to keep," she said with a smile. "You should hang a sign in town saying you're training horses. I bet different men would bring you their horse so you could help it to fulfill its destiny."

"That's not a bad idea. I'll ask Pa if it would be all right if I made a sign like that and put it up in the store. I know Jensen won't mind."

"That's a really good idea," she said.

He laughed. "It was yours!"

"That must be why it was so good," she said, winking at him.

He sat down and looked at his eggs. He was very particular about the yolk being totally cooked. "Looks perfect," he said.

She took her seat beside him and joined her hands with his for their prayer. "I'd like to go into town with you when you go," she said. "If you don't mind."

"I don't," he said. "Are you looking for something in particular?"

She nodded. "I feel like all my dresses are falling apart. Even my Sunday best needs to become a work dress. I'd love to get some fabric to make a new dress or two."

"Get enough for three," he said. "You work hard, and you deserve to have pretty dresses. Emma might help you make them."

"Is she a good seamstress?" Abby had always been good at making her own clothes, but she'd never enjoyed it. Perhaps she could trade chores with Emma.

"Oh, yes. She's wonderful at it."

"I'll talk to her then." She'd be willing to scrub Emma's house from top to bottom or even cook for her and Jared for a week or two. Anything so she didn't have to waste her time sewing.

"All right," he said. As soon as they'd finished eating, he put on his hat and pulled a coat on. "I'm going to run and talk to Pa. I'm sure he'll think it's a good idea."

"How many horses would you like to do at one time?" she asked.

He shrugged. "Ideally four or five. Then I could do a morning and afternoon session with each every day. I'll be back!" He hurried out the door, and she stood staring at it momentarily before laughing. The man was always so focused on what he wanted or needed to do he didn't remember the social niceties. He probably didn't think he needed to remember them with his wife.

He came back as she was finishing up the dishes. "He said that's fine as long as we don't take too long. There's lots to be done today, and he wants me to be able to spend my last two hours training Skunk."

She wiped her hands on her apron, taking it off, and pulling a shawl off a peg by the door. She threw it over her shoulders, and said, "I'm ready."

He leaned down and kissed the tip of her nose. She couldn't help but smile. It was a new thing for him to show her affection when he wasn't wanting to go to bed with her. She liked it more than she could express.

They hurried out to the wagon he'd hitched up after talking to his father. "Let's go!"

He drove a little faster than she would have liked down the steep hill into town. It was a straight shot down to the mercantile, and he stopped in front. "I forgot to make a sign!" he said, hitting the back of his head with the heel of his hand.

"I'm sure Mr. Jensen will have something you can use."

Inside, Mrs. Jensen was at the counter. Abby knew her from church, but as this was only her second time in the store, she'd not seen her there before. She walked straight to the sweet woman. "Bastian and I came to town so he could put up a sign, and then he forgot to make it. We're in a hurry and don't want to return home. Do you have a piece of paper and pen he can use?"

Penelope Jensen nodded, holding a baby on one hip as she reached for paper. "Do the shopping you want to do. I'll help Bastian."

"Thank you!" Abby really liked Penelope but had little time to talk to her. Thankfully, they were going to start having a quilting circle every Wednesday afternoon now that gardens were in. She made a mental note to talk to Penelope when she got the chance.

Looking through the yard goods, Abby found three fabrics that she really liked. She also chose some white fabric so she could make another nightgown and an apron. Once Bastian was working on his note, she called Penelope over to cut the fabric. "Thank you for all your help today," Abby said. "Mr. Appleby wants Bastian back quickly so he can work. They just got in from the cattle drive last night."

"Oh!" Penelope said. "How did the cattle drive go?"

"They made a good amount more per head than they expected to," Abby said with a smile. "We have some very happy men around the ranch."

Penelope smiled. "I'm glad to hear it. They are so easy to work with. I need to buy another side of beef soon," she said.

"I'm sure they'll be more than happy to accommodate you. They kept some of the steer back for the next year's butchering."

"They're smart men."

Soon, Bastian and Abby were on their way back up the hill. "How'd the sign turn out?" she asked. She hadn't taken the time to look at it when he was done.

"Good, I hope. I put it on the board at the back of the store. That's where everyone goes if they're looking to buy or sell something." He glanced over at her, taking his eyes off the road for just a moment. "What do you have planned for the day?" he asked.

"I'm going to talk to Emma and beg her to trade chores with me. We'll see how that goes. We're all meeting up at Emma's this morning."

"Are you going to ask her to make the dress?"

"I am. I'll do whatever she needs in exchange."

"Sounds fair to me," Bastian said, stopping the wagon in front of their cabin and jumping down to unhitch the wagon.

Abby took the fabric from the back of the wagon and carried it with her to Emma's house. To Abby's surprise, she was the first one there. "I have a huge favor to ask."

Emma looked up from where she was kneading dough to get it ready to rise. "What's that?"

"Bastian said you're an excellent seamstress. I was hoping if I did some of your chores for a while, you would make three dresses for me."

Emma nodded. "You don't even have to do my chores."

Abby frowned. "I can't accept it if you don't let me work it off."

"All right." Emma looked around as if she was trying to find something that needed doing.

"Why don't I start with your laundry? I'll strip the bed and wash it all, and I'll bake your bread as well."

Emma nodded. "All right."

Abby got started stripping the bed and pulled down the curtains as well. "I'll just make sure to wash these as well. How long has it been since your floor was scrubbed?"

Emma laughed. "Since before the men left, but no one's been here."

"I'll do that when I'm done hanging the clothes and kneading the bread."

"All right." Emma spread the fabric out on the dining table. She'd been taught that most dresses needed to be made the same size. That way, it would fit whether a woman was pregnant or not and would fit through feast and famine. She took out scissors and started cutting immediately.

Abby sang as she hung the clothes on the line. She was so much happier cleaning than she was sewing.

Chapter Ten

B y November, a thick blanket of snow was on the ground, turning the beautiful green landscape into a winter wonderland. Emma had completed all three of Abby's dresses, but Abby had waited to wear them. Bastian had promised her a sleigh ride on Sunday, and she was looking forward to it.

They were settling into something of a cold weather routine. She and the other ladies still got together every day, but there were no longer foods to can or gardens to harvest, so they moved from house to house, and all the women worked on projects together.

Mostly they quilted or sewed, but because Abby hated to sew more than she hated anything else in the world, she spent her time knitting instead. She knitted scarves, hats, and mittens for all the men in the family and some booties for the baby Emma was expecting.

Abby kept praying for a baby but hadn't been rewarded yet. Soon, she hoped. Of course, her mother had wanted many children, but she'd only had Abby. Perhaps that would be how things would go with her as she tried to get pregnant.

The joy and laughter she felt day after day was immeasurable. Sometimes the other women would laugh about something Bastian had said or done, but Abby kept quiet. To her, Bastian seemed to live in another world, away from the rest of them. He was generally content with life, but there were times when it all became too much for him, and he had to step away to be alone. There were now church socials on the first Saturday night of each month, and Abby looked forward to them, though she knew Bastian may not be able to remain inside for the entire event.

On the Saturdays when they didn't go to a church social, one of the women would host the entire family for a game of cards. They'd split up into teams and play hand after hand. The game they all loved was Euchre, and they all enjoyed it. Sometimes there was a baby at the table with them, and sometimes they all slept. It didn't seem to matter which way it went for their entertainment level.

On the second Saturday of November, Henri announced she was expecting again. Her face was positively glowing as she talked about it, and Roy seemed to be a proud papa.

While she was happy for Henri, Abby was also sad. She wanted a baby of her own. Henri already had one. Why wasn't it her turn?

"Just don't let your stepmother get pregnant again!" Pa had called out. "I have five children, and that should be enough for anyone."

Henri laughed. "I think you're more in control of that than I am, Pa."

Abby felt like everyone was staring at her for not being pregnant, but when she looked up from her cards, everyone was looking at Henri. Maybe no one thought she'd ever get pregnant, and maybe they were right!

She wanted to break down and cry, but there was no reason. No, she would bide her time, and surely God would bless her and Bastian with their own child.

She was quieter than usual for the rest of the night, wondering why some people were so blessed when others were left wanting.

After they finished playing for the night, she and Bastian walked home to the pie she had waiting for him. He didn't know about it, but she knew he'd be pleased. The man couldn't turn down a pie if his life depended on it.

Once home, she cut the pie, carried it to the table, and set it down. Then she fetched two plates and forks, and two glasses of milk. While they ate, Bastian watched her closely.

Finally, he said, "I'm not good at reading faces or knowing what people are thinking, but you seem awfully sad tonight. Is something wrong?"

She started to shake her head, but then she thought it was better to open up to him. "I'm just sad that it was Henri announcing she was expecting tonight and not us."

He put his hand on top of hers. "It'll happen. We've only been married for six weeks and half of those we spent at Pa's place and nothing happened between us. I'm sure it'll happen soon."

Abby felt a tear drip down her cheek, and she swiped it away angrily. She was much too old to sit and cry over apple pie. "I'm sorry. I was really hoping it would happen."

He nodded. "I also want a baby, but I don't think stressing over it will make it happen. Do you want to see the doctor and make sure nothing is wrong?"

She shook her head immediately. "No, there's no reason for that. It hasn't been long enough to worry about, but I'm borrowing trouble."

"Yes, you are," he said, "but if you want to see the doctor, I'll take you."

She shook her head. "No, we don't need to do that. I'm just glad you're not angry that it hasn't happened yet."

"Angry? Seriously? I get to play with my playground longer if you're not expecting yet."

His face was so serious as he said the words that Abby couldn't hold back a laugh. "You make me really happy, Bastian. I love you."

Bastian looked at her for a moment, and finally said, "Thank you."

Abby wanted to ask how he felt about her, but she knew Bastian too well to do that. If he needed more time before he knew that he loved her, then she'd give it to him. She wanted him to be sure when he eventually told her he loved her anyway.

After church the following morning, they had their Sunday dinner, and then Bastian hitched up the sleigh. "Where are we taking it?" she asked.

He shrugged. "I thought I'd just go wherever the horses took me. I love long drives on snowy days."

"All right!" she bundled up as well as she could and carried a thick quilt out to the sleigh to rest across their laps. The sleigh was tightly built, and they sat completely pressed up against one another on the seat.

He drove down the hill and then they headed out toward the lake. She didn't ask again where they were going because he obviously had something in mind. After an hour or two, she realized they'd bypassed the lake, and they were heading up a mountain across the lake from where they lived.

Finally, they made it to the top, and they could look out over the lake and see the hill they lived on, if not make out their home. Bastian got out of the sleigh and held his hand down for Abby's. When she got out, he wrapped his arms around her from behind. "I think this is the most beautiful place in the whole area," he said softly.

She smiled and nodded. "I've never seen anything like it."

"When I asked you to go for a sleigh ride with me, I had no idea where I intended to go. I was thinking more about whipping around the valley together, and maybe visiting a couple of friends. But last night, when you told me you loved me, I knew this is where we needed to come. It felt so good to hear you say the words, that I realized you would feel good if you heard them as well."

Abby's heart beat faster at the idea that he would tell her how much he cared. It felt good to know he was even thinking about it. "Yes."

"So, I brought you here, because there's not a more beautiful place in all the world to tell my wife that I love her with every fiber of my being. I've known for a long time I felt that way, but I didn't think it mattered if I said them. Last night, you taught me differently, so I'm standing here, on this mountain, looking over the valley, to tell you how much I love you. I didn't know loving someone as much as I love you was possible. And now that we're here, I feel like I can't stop."

She turned in his arms and looked at him. His brown eyes were staring deeply into her own. He was odd, but that was all right. She loved everything about him, and she always would. "I love you too, Bastian, and I never want you to stop. You make me laugh, and smile, and you make me a better person."

"You make me pies!" he said.

Abby felt the laugh rumbling up from deep within her. "I will always make you pies. I know that you need them to stay happy, and no woman could ever be satisfied with an unhappy man!"

"And there'll be new kinds of pie in the spring!" he said. "I don't know if I could ever tell you how much I love the pies you make."

"You don't even have to try. I can see it on your face every time you take a bite."

"How did I get so lucky to get you in trade for just six oxen? You are a one-hundred oxen woman if there ever was one."

As they drove back, she was filled with happiness. Bastian loved her back, and for more than just her pies. He loved her for her. It was a very nice thing to hear.

Before bed that night, she put on her new nightgown that Emma had made for her, not realizing just how flimsy the thing was. It was sleeveless, and there was lace all over the bodice, which was beautiful, but also revealing. She walked to the table to stand beside Bastian, who was reading another book on horse training. He ordered them from the mercantile whenever he heard there was a new one out.

"Are you ready for bed?" she asked.

He glanced up from his book, and instead of saying, "Just let me finish this chapter" as he usually did, he put a piece of paper to mark his page, his gaze on the lace covering her bosom.

He swooped her up into his arms and carried her into the bedroom, dropping her on the bed. "I remember you saying something about wanting a baby," he said. "Is that still the case?"

She lay on the bed watching him divest himself of clothing faster than ever. He hadn't even bothered to turn down the lamp in the main room. When he was completely naked, she whispered, "You should turn down the lamp."

He looked over his shoulder and grunted, walking back into the main room, shutting off the light, and returning to their bedroom, shutting the door behind him.

"Now, let's see about making that baby!"

Epilogue

It took longer for them to make a baby than either Abby or Bastian anticipated. In late May, Abby realized she'd missed her cycle for the past two months. She sat at the kitchen table after cooking a breakfast that she hadn't been able to keep down and counted on her fingers.

When she realized she was expecting, it was all she could do not to jump up and down. Of course, doing so would have led to her getting sick again, so she decided not to make any sudden movements.

Instead, she sat there for a few minutes, just thinking of names she liked. She knew it was early, but the baby needed a name.

Instead of walking to Melody's house where they were all meeting that morning to plant their new garden, she walked to the stable. There, she saw Bastian working with a new foal. She tapped Bastian on the shoulder.

He spun to face her after jumping. "Don't do that!"

She grinned. "Sorry."

"Are you feeling better?" he asked.

"Not really, but that's all right."

"No, it's not all right. I'll hitch up the wagon and take you to see the doctor."

"There's no need," she said. "I know what's wrong with me. Or rather that there's nothing wrong with me."

"If you're sick to your stomach, then something is wrong!" he insisted.

"Not if I'm expecting!"

He stood looking at her momentarily before gathering her in his arms. His first instinct was to spin her in a circle, but he didn't particularly want the contents of her stomach coming back up again. "Are you sure?"

She nodded. "I'm sure. I'll see Mrs. Mitchell later this week, but I'm sure."

His smile seemed to stretch from ear to ear. "We're having a baby!" he shouted.

"Well, now I guess we don't have to do a big announcement because the whole ranch knows already."

He chuckled. "Maybe I shouldn't yell about it, but we've been trying for so long!"

"I guess we finally got it right!"

He pressed his lips to her ear and whispered something she was glad no one else heard. "I can't think of anyone I'd rather try with," she said, her face lit with laughter.

"I love you, Abby Appleby. I don't ever want you to forget it!"

"Oh, I won't. But my name sounds silly, so don't say the two together anymore, all right?"

He laughed. "It does sound funny. I guess I should have told you my last name before I married you."

She shrugged. "It wouldn't have mattered. You were willing to pay six oxen for me, so there's no way my father would have let me back out of the wedding."

"Silly man. You were worth at least a thousand."

Abby smiled, resting her head on his shoulder. "Only you would say so."

Milton Keynes UK
Ingram Content Group UK Ltd.
UKHW040702151023
430644UK00001B/2